MW00807302

THE LAST OLE SOUTHERN SHERIFF

Jeffery P. Duval

First Edition

NEWMAN SPRINGS PUBLISHING
320 Broad Street
Red Bank, NJ 07701

First originally published by Newman Springs Publishing 2021

Names, characters, places and some incidents are used fictitiously and any resemblance to actual persons, living or dead, business establishments, events or locales is entirely coincidental, or used with the written consent of the parties or their heirs.

This book was written with the assistance of Traci Drummond Bush and Diane Byrd.

ISBN 978-1-63881-125-1 (Paperback)
ISBN 978-1-63881-126-8 (Hardcover)
ISBN 978-1-63881-127-5 (Digital)

Printed in the United States of America

To the men and women of law enforcement
who gave their lives in the line of duty

ACKNOWLEDGMENT

A special thanks to David M. Newell, author of *The Trouble of It Is* and *If Nothin' Don't Happen*, who invited and met with me at his home, in Lake County, Florida, and shared his knowledge in the writing of this book before his passing.

Also, a special thanks to Johnny McDaniel, aka Johnny Mac, longtime sheriff of Jackson County, Florida, author of *the High Sheriff*, a longtime friend, whose wife was murdered just before his retirement, after serving thirty years in law enforcement. His book is a must-read.

A special thanks to Sheriff Sim L. Lowman, Sheriff Melvin R. Kelly, and Sheriff Jamie Adams.

A special thanks to Ernie and Nancy Chatman Sr. for helping to mentor me from the age of fourteen. They were family to me and treated me like one of their own children. Dad told me the night Lonnie Colburn was murdered, as we were riding along looking for the killers, that he loved me like his own sons. He was Dad and she was Mom!

A special thanks and love to my granddaddy Robert "Bob" R. Glass and my grandmother Effie Glass and with love and gratitude also to my mother, Jacqueline.

A special thanks to my immediate family, my wife, and my children, Jeff Duval II and Avery Lynn Duval, for their understanding and patience and the long hours of being away from home. Some of the work I did they were never told for their safety's sake!

HOW IT ALL BEGAN

. . . .

Thinking back on it, at fifteen years old, little did Jeff Duval know that a happenstance evening he and a small group of friends decided to go to a basketball game at Hernando High School, after being invited by Billy and Pam, their best friends. It just so happened that his future wife and the mother of his children, Bobbie, decided to go along with the group. Jeff and Bobbie spent a lot of time talking and getting to know each other better at the dance. From that night forward, they were inseparable. They knew it was meant to be. It was like something magical happened that night. A few years later, Bobbie and Jeff eloped and were married, which angered Bobbie's father, who just happened to be Jeff's boss at a local GM Car Dealership; and of course, he fired Jeff immediately and told him to find a job and support his wife. Jeff did just that. Some prominent friends of Jeff's family in the county gave him a job at the Brooksville Rock Company in Brooksville. A few years later, Jeff and Bobbie had two fine sons, Jeffery and Avery Duval.

Jeff enjoyed his job at the mine working on heavy equipment and was eager to learn how to run all the equipment he could. The days were hot and very dusty and sometimes very cold and muddy. He had a lot of respect for his foreman, Mr. Fred Farmer, who was a big man in many ways. He had a good relationship with Jeff and invited him to join the Leopard Athletic Club that he belonged to himself. Jeff was happy to join his ole alma mater with several other businessmen in town.

After working a few years of hard labor and very dangerous working surroundings in the mines, it was a pleasant surprise when one evening after supper, just around six o'clock, Bobbie's mother called and asked Bobbie if she could speak to Jeff. Bobbie handed the telephone to Jeff and said, "Mom wants to talk to you." Her mother asked Jeff if he would like to come back to work at the GM Car Dealership. Jeff thought Bobbie's father believed he had paid his dues and was a man of his word. Jeff figured he'd had time to cool down.

After going back to work for them, they became as close as father and son over the years. Jeff called him Dad and Bobbie's mother, Mom, until the day they died. He loved them both with all his heart and still misses them today, some forty-five years later.

Jeff was seventeen years old and had experienced more in his young life than most people had. That's how he met the "high sheriff" of Hernando County, Florida, at Dad's car dealership. He already knew of the sheriff's no-nonsense reputation as a hard-nosed man with an air about him that many in the community feared. At six feet, five inches and three hundred pounds of stature, dark hair, and the look of an American Indian, it was not hard to understand the fear he put into some people.

When the sheriff drove into the car dealership and got out of his car on a Friday afternoon in October 1968, Jeff summoned all the strength he could muster and walked over to where the high sheriff was standing.

Jeff said, "Hello, Sheriff. How's it going?"

The sheriff replied, "Need an oil change, boy, and don't forget to check the tires."

That was Jeff's first close encounter with Sheriff Sim Lowman, "Sim L." to most of Hernando County. Jeff watched as the sheriff walked away without another word.

The sheriff and Dad had been hunting buddies from way back. They shared a hunting camp in the Gulf Hammock area on the west coast of Florida. Wild Turkey Whiskey and wild stories were probably more prevalent around the campfires than the game they were hunting in the daytime.

Many deputies came into the shop to have their patrol cars serviced, and Jeff got to know all seven of them. One Friday, Deputy Lamar Chapman came into the shop to have his patrol car serviced.

Jeff asked, "Lamar, do you think I might ride with you tonight to the football game?"

Lamar replied, "Sure! Just ask your mom," with a snicker as he walked away.

Jeff laughed and said, "Lamar, I will meet you at the sheriff's office about six thirty this evening."

Jeff remembered the feeling of excitement riding around in that patrol car not knowing what was going to happen next. It was on that night he realized he wanted to experience more of that excitement and wanted a future in law enforcement. As soon as Jeff could, he signed up to be a volunteer with the Hernando County Sheriff's Office to learn the ropes and to have more opportunities to ride along. He started volunteering in the office. He had no way of knowing that the long road ahead would be filled with good times and hard times, but his passion for helping people who were down on their luck and couldn't help themselves and seeing justice served would give him the desire to keep going.

In October 1969, Jeff went to work full time in the sheriff's office. After working in the office for two years, he went to Saint Leo State College for basic training and earned his blue line certificate. He was eager to get back to work at the sheriff's office.

One afternoon when things were kind of quiet, he was in the office when the big man walked out and said those dreaded words, "Boy, let me see you in my office." At this point, all the things he might have done wrong were racing through his mind. Was he going to get one of those fist-pounding, stern, lip-biting lectures or what? As Jeff came through the door, the sheriff was standing behind his big wooden desk, with a stern look on his face. He stopped at the desk, and the sheriff looked him straight in the eyes and threw a deputy sheriff's badge on the desk while saying, "Put that on you, SOB."

Jeff replied, "What do you mean by that, Sheriff?"

The sheriff said, "Boy, from this day on, you are going to find out who your real friends are. You will go on the road Monday morning at six o'clock till."

Jeff asked him, "Till what?"

The sheriff answered, "When you put that star on, there ain't no starting time and there ain't no quitting time, till the job is done. You will be working a minimum of seventy-two hours a week for $350 a month with one day off, unless I need you out."

Little did Jeff realize at that time, he would work a hot case for two or three days and nights only to go home to eat, shower, and go back out. But he wanted to be like Deputy Melvin Kelly, a bulldog, stay out, track them down, and dog them till they would drop or give up knowing that he was on their heels. Mel was low-key until he was fired up. Sometimes the Irish came busting out. Jeff always watched him walk in the door every morning at five forty-five. Mel would shuffle around the counter as he would pick up the paper and head for the coffee pot; if you spoke to him or if he grunted or said, "Morning," it was okay. If not, you better get the hell out of the office, quick.

Jeff remembered one morning Mel fired a deputy for lying to him. A few days later, while they were out on a case, Jeff asked him why he fired the deputy that day. Mel said, "He lied to me. You cannot trust a liar. Don't ever lie to me, Jeff. If you make a mistake, tell me the truth, and I will work with that if I can. But if you lie, then you're gone." That statement was taken to heart. There were a few times that Jeff thought that he would possibly be reprimanded for something that he had done or a mistake in judgment. Even though he feared that he would let Mel down, he still would man up and confess his bad judgments. Mel had a certain look that needed no explanation, and it was a "you better keep on the straight and narrow path" look. Jeff would walk out, wipe off his brow, and give a sigh of relief that he was not reprimanded. Mel would later confess that he had made the same mistakes early in his career.

Jeff finally got to go through basic training with the Florida Department of Law Enforcement Training in Tallahassee. He also attended training with the Federal Bureau of Investigations and graduated near the top of his class and was trained in hand-to-hand combat and SWAT, firing range and qualified as a sniper and earned the combat master pin, the highest pin you can earn on the firing range. Jeff had a natural eye when it came to shooting in combat situations on the FBI course. He loved the challenges of the course. He finished with honors. During his career, he continued his education in law enforcement by attending various colleges in the state. One of those colleges was Saint Leo in San Antonio, Florida. One of those classes was the sex crime class, which was held in the basement of the girls' dormitory. While there, Jeff always wondered how a pair of girl's panties ended up on the FBI instructor's podium while the class was out to lunch. Everyone had a big laugh when the instructor walked in and didn't notice the new decoration on his podium.

In 1971, Sheriff Sim L. Lowman had served since 1949. The county had changed from a small mining and citrus town into a large populated county in a short period of years. No more a small Southern town. The Yankees had retaken the South, most moving to the west side nearer to the Gulf of Mexico. Unfortunately, the sheriff's department wasn't funded enough to keep up with the growth. The department had grown from seven deputies to fifteen deputies and was still short of the state and federal guidelines that stated one officer per thousand citizens. Hernando County was the fastest-growing county in the state, and the deputies were running about four thousand citizens per deputy. Jeff was a road sergeant during this time with a five-man squad. He and his squad were answering thirty calls per day, without having a lunch break or having a restroom break. Jeff remembered one morning the calls were backed up after he had worked a large burglary case in Spring Hill. He remembered when he checked back on 10-8 on the burglary, the dispatcher advised, "Sarge, we have five more calls pending at this time." Jeff remembered throwing the microphone to the floor and saying to himself, *How in the hell are you supposed to do a job correctly when you don't have the officers?* The department was under a lot of stress, and the ole sheriff found himself in a firestorm with the newcomers.

Jeff heard rumors of Deputy Melvin Kelly and Red Brass possibly running for sheriff in the fall of 1971. Melvin Kelly had been hired by Lowman in 1955, and it was only a three-man department at that time. Melvin Kelly was a hard-nosed Irish Southerner and was the best crime-fighting, bad-man-catching bulldog of a deputy sheriff that Jeff had ever seen, but Melvin also had a soft spot for the victims of the crimes and showed the bad guy little mercy.

One morning about daybreak, Jeff and Melvin were standing on the ole colonial Southern front porch of the sheriff's office. Melvin looked straight ahead and said, "I guess you heard that I will be running for sheriff in the fall."

Jeff swallowed hard and replied, "Yep, I heard." It was news he really didn't want to hear, because he liked all three men and knew that this wasn't going down good with the big sheriff.

Melvin turned and looked Jeff straight in the eye and asked, "What are you going to do?"

Jeff looked straight at Melvin and said, "I have always respected you and Red and we have been close. There is no one that I have respected more. I must be loyal to the badge, not the man. Sheriff Lowman gave me my start. If I quit him now, how would you know that I might not stab you in the back down the road? I cannot politic, Mel. I work for the people of Hernando County. However, I will be loyal to the end if you are elected."

Nelson "Red" Brass was a local rancher and a good man. In my opinion, politics has no friends. However, the Northerners didn't care. Melvin Kelly won by a landslide in the fall.

On January 1, 1972, Melvin Kelly walked up the front steps at a quarter till midnight with a large group of supporters and followers behind him. Jeff was working that night and witnessed history in Hernando County. The changing of the old guard and a new era was beginning. He was happy and sad at the same time. Melvin stayed just inside the front door with his men behind him. At ten minutes to midnight, the ole sheriff walked out of his office and looked around and then said, like he had said many times before, "Mel, let me see you in my office." Exactly at midnight the ole sheriff walked out smiling. He stopped when he came to Jeff and shook his hand saying, "Boy, I guess we'll have to find a job."

Jeff said, "Thanks, Sheriff, for giving me a start." The ole sheriff walked out into the night, and Melvin and Sim were never seen together again.

The crowd milled around the office not knowing what to expect next. The new sheriff took command at that moment and started giving directives to certain people that he handpicked to serve on his staff. Jeff wondered where he was going to serve since he did not politic for either man. A meeting was called in the conference room, and Jeff casually walked into the meeting, stood against the wall, and gave the new sheriff a thumbs-up.

Sheriff Kelly started his new position by ordering an inventory of the department and informing the staff that some would be relieved that night and some would find their fate in the newspaper on Monday. The new sheriff said, "If your name is on the list in the newspaper, then you will be retained." Some staff members, who had worked for Sheriff Lowman for a short period of time, was let go that night.

Jeff remembered what Mel Kelly had told him on the front porch on a cool morning a year ago. Jeff remained loyal to the job and the people of Hernando County and rose to the rank of first sergeant. He stayed with Sheriff Kelly for three terms, through the good and the bad. God knows there was plenty of both. When Jeff got down or depressed about the job, he would go to the sheriff's farm and talk to him. They had a father-and-son type of relationship, and he would feel better when he left the farm. Melvin once told Jeff, "Don't worry about things so much. The bad passes just like the good."

Sometime around 1975 to 1980, the chief deputy and Sheriff Melvin Kelly were summoned out of state on a major case. Sheriff Kelly appointed Sgt. Jeff Duval as acting sheriff until his return one week later.

That afternoon as Jeff pulled away from the gas pump on Jefferson Street, he realized what a great responsibility he had been handed as he drove away from the ole colonial building that housed the sheriff's office during that era and thought what a burden he had been handed. Not many people realize the weight of a sheriff's badge and the responsibilities that go along with it. Jeff suddenly did as he looked over at the sheriff's office, as he drove away heading west out of town. He prayed to God to stand with him until the sheriff returned.

It was a normal week without incidences. Jeff was thankful to the good Lord that everything went well.

He had a great respect for the authority and weight of the badge the high sheriff wore in those days. The chief deputy is the undersheriff, while the deputies are the right hand of the sheriff.

Sheriff Melvin Kelly knew that the times were changing with the rapid growth in Hernando County. He had more than enough time in after serving three terms and serving the citizens of Hernando County and retired comfortably on his farm and decided not to run for reelection again because he wanted to go out undefeated. Sheriff Kelly had moved the sheriff's department forward from the old ways and lived happily on his farm for several years until he fell ill.

On Sheriff Kelly's last day in office, after serving three terms, Jeff turned his resignation letter in to Sheriff Kelly. In the letter of resignation, Jeff thanked the citizens of Hernando County for allowing him to serve them for approximately fifteen years.

Jeff was immediately hired by Sheriff Jamie Adams in Sumter County. Jeff and Jamie had been friends for many years since the time Jamie worked for the state as a game warden.

After three years working for the Sumter County Sheriff's Office, Jeff Duval was offered a job in Port St. Joe, Gulf County, Florida, where his father's family had lived for over eight generations. Sheriff Harrison offered Jeff a lieutenant's position, third in command, at the Gulf County Sheriff's Office. Jeff was delighted to be back in Northwest Florida and the Gulf of Mexico after so many years of being away. He took great pride in riding by and seeing the large monument that depicted his great-great-great-granddaddy, the first territorial governor of Florida, William P. Duval. His roots run deep in the Florida soil.

Jeff and Sheriff Melvin Kelly remained close friends until the night he died. Jeff was by Melvin's bedside that night, along with Melvin's daughter, Melba, and Deputy Cliff Batten. Jeff loved the old man and had a great respect for him and his wife, Louise. The sheriff had stuck by his side through many hard times throughout his career. Jeff stood there and rubbed his head trying to relax the ole sheriff, as he lay in a hospital bed at Lykes Memorial Hospital. Jeff said, with tears running down his cheeks, "I'm here, Homer. Rest now and go home," as the sheriff was taking his last breaths. Melvin was more than a boss or sheriff to Jeff. Jeff remembered "Homer" was a nickname that Deputy Richard Clay gave the sheriff one afternoon long ago while standing on the old front porch at the sheriff's office joking around. Jeff never thought that would be the last thing that he would ever say to his old friend, Sheriff Melvin Kelly, whom he had known since he was five years old. Friends like that do not come along very often.

It angered and saddened Jeff, after his retirement in the mid-1990s, and after moving back to Hernando County, and out of curiosity, to find out by going through his personnel file at the Hernando County Sheriff's Office, the sheriff that had been elected after Sheriff Kelly's retirement, had written in his personnel file that Jeff had retired from the Hernando County Sheriff's Office, which was not true. Jeff had not retired—he simply resigned. All letters of accommodation had been removed, and the file was all but expunged by the new sheriff, who had a strong dislike for Sergeant Duval because of Jeff's loyalty and strong ties to Sheriff Kelly.

Jeff knew in his heart that was the kind of politics the new sheriff would play. Jeff had honed his political skills over the years and knew that he did not care to work for a sheriff wearing a three-piece suit.

It was with great pleasure and honor to be hired by Sheriff Jamie Adams of Sumter County, Florida. Sheriff Adams was a very honorable man, and Jeff had a great deal of respect for Sheriff Adams.

When Jeff was hired by Gulf County, he told Sheriff Adams the only reason he was leaving was to be near his family back in West Florida and thanked Sheriff Jamie Adams for sticking by him through some hard times.

As the years passed by, Jeff knew "what goes around eventually comes back around," and it finally did. Jeff once said that, after everything was said and done, he took no pleasure in seeing Sheriff Millinder suffer because some of his best friends had betrayed him in the end.

DEATH OF A SPECIAL DEPUTY

Bill Langston was a part-time special deputy sheriff with the Hernando County Sheriff's Office in the early 1950s. Some of these special deputies were volunteers, and some were paid for the hours they worked part-time.

This is a story that will always haunt me because of the way Deputy Bill Langston died serving the citizens of Hernando County, just like any other deputy that wore a badge.

As the story unfolds, Langston was taken to a local area by then Sheriff Sim L. Lowman. I believe it was around the Horse Lake area, where it was said that moonshine whiskey was being sold. Sheriff Sim L. Lowman had heard that a local black man was selling the shine from his house and asked Langston to accompany him out to the site. The two men observed whiskey being sold from the moonshiner's house.

Sheriff Lowman decided that he would get a warrant to search the residence and surrounding area. He told Langston to stay and keep an eye on the moonshiner and residence until he could obtain a solid search warrant. Sheriff Lowman drove back to Brooksville to the local judge's home. He obtained the search warrant and then he drove back to the area of Horse Lake where several black families lived, surrounded by orange groves and woods. The sheriff parked his car and made his way back on foot to where Langston was hiding behind a log so he could keep an eye on the moonshiner and what was going on at the site.

As Sheriff Lowman approached the area, he found Special Deputy Bill Langston lying dead from a gunshot wound. It is believed at this time Sheriff Lowman went back to town to summon more help and returned to the scene to arrest the bootleggers.

Once they arrived at the sheriff's office in Brooksville with the bootleggers, it is said they were questioned where a witness testified after a coroner's jury was summoned. The name of the man that was arrested slips my mind, as my memory fails me, but I remember the story being told to me by Chief Deputy Red Brass in the early 1970s.

Time marched on! Chief Deputy Red Brass retired in 1969. Deputy Melvin Kelly became chief deputy under Sheriff Sim L. Lowman in 1970, as my memory serves me. Langston began to fade away like the bark on a sycamore tree that falls away every year. People come, and people go, as do sheriffs, but stories told by the ole Southern sheriffs will live on as long as I live. I am privileged to be able to share some of these stories that I have witnessed and was told about.

Now, as far as new sheriffs, like I said, they came, and they went. They lived and died just like everyone else will.

In 1971, Sheriff Deputy Melvin Kelly ran against his boss, Sim L. Lowman, and won by a landslide. Thus came the name Landslide Kelly. The people of Hernando County wanted a change. Time marched on! So do the memories fade further away of Special Deputy Bill Langston, except in the memory of a young deputy sheriff, Jeff Duval.

Jeff, at the time this book was written, had a hard time understanding why Langston never received recognition for his sacrifice to the people of Hernando County. After all, he was wearing a Hernando County badge at the time of his death. He was working for Hernando County. Time marches on!

Sheriff Melvin Kelly began to bring the sheriff's office up to date with the changing times. In 1971, Hernando County was the fastest-growing county in Florida with a population boom from the north. Kelly served three terms as sheriff. Melvin Kelly never received recognition for the changes and the improvements he implemented during the fast-changing times that kept marching on! Langston's memory fades further away.

In 1984, Sheriff Melvin Kelly retired undefeated, as time marched on. Sgt. Jeff Duval transferred to Sumter County in 1984 and then to Gulf County as third in command in 1988, with heavy responsibilities and approximately fifty people under his command. Stress began to take a toll after losing five friends in the line of duty over the years. In mid-1995, he was injured in a drug buy that went bad on Highway 98, just outside Port St. Joe, Florida, and was nearly beaten to death after being dragged into the swamp by a very large drug dealer and a Mexican. He was taken to the Bay Memorial Hospital in Panama City, Florida, due to the injuries he had sustained and was later transported to a Rivendale Rehab Center, where he spent a few more weeks recovering.

While in rehab, Dr. John Redick told him one evening that he was no longer fit to carry on with his duties because of the physical and mental injuries that he had sustained. As Dr. John Redick spoke the words, Jeff could hear him, but his heart could not accept the fact that his long law enforcement career was over. He could feel the warm tears streaming down his face. He remembered his daddy coming to his room the next morning and repeating what the doctor had said. Jeff told his dad he wanted to stay on for a few more years. After all, he had been in law enforcement all his adult life serving the people.

His dad said, "Son, you can't save the world. Accept this and get out while you are still alive." Jeff took the advice of his doctors and family and accepted his fate. He had done all he could do to serve and protect the people he worked for, the people of Florida. Time marches on!

There were only two more things Jeff wished to accomplish before his time was up. One was to write these stories and to leave them with the people that he loved so much so they would not be lost in time, like Bill Langston's memory. The second thing was to remind the people of Hernando County, Florida, and whoever the sheriff may be at the time of this writing, to remember Special Deputy Sheriff Bill Langston, who gave his life while serving the people of Hernando County, Florida.

Currently, there are three names on the Memorial Wall at the Hernando County Sheriff's Office in Brooksville. Two of these men, Jeff watched grow up in Hernando County. They all three served with honor. Bill Langston's name, it is my feeling, should be placed on the Memorial Wall at the Hernando County Sheriff's Office, as he died serving under Sheriff Sim L. Lowman, doing what he was commanded to do by the sheriff. He is no less deserving.

There had been three sheriffs who served in Hernando County since Melvin Kelly's retirement. I hope in the near future, one good man as sheriff will step forward and do the right thing by adding Special Deputy Bill Langston's name to the Memorial Wall at the sheriff's office in Brooksville, Florida. If not, may God have mercy on the officials of Hernando County, Florida.

BIG JAIL BREAK

The afternoon was like any other. Cecil came in about five thirty in the afternoon to relieve Ronnie, the day shift dispatcher and jailer. Back in the early 1970s, dispatcher and correction officers worked twelve-hour shifts or nights. After going through the afternoon paperwork, Ronnie was getting ready to leave, and Cecil was settling down in the dispatch chair.

Cecil asked, "Is there anything else that I need to know?"

Ronnie answered, "No. I'll see you in the morning."

Now if you've ever been in Florida in August, you know how hot and humid it is. Okay!

The evening started off smoothly as Cecil settled in, attending all four phone lines, three radios, and a teletype machine. After getting the prisoners fed and settled into their night cells, one of the road deputies came in to get a cup of "jailhouse coffee." We just called him "Burr Head."

Now ole Burr Head was a little strange in some ways. He would talk to you and roll his eyes up to the left instead of looking at you when he talked and rubbed his burr head.

Cecil finally said, "Burr Head, I have a feeling the sheriff is out tonight."

With that, Burr Head said, "I better hit the road then," and with that, he was gone.

Now, along about a quarter to ten, ole Cecil was sitting around the radio and thinking about how quite it was that night. Just about that time, he heard a lot of commotion after seeing a big truck pull down beside the jail and stop alongside the jail wall.

Now Cecil was known to get excited. He was thinking, *What is that truck doing stopping alongside of the jail?* He put the radio on hold after telling all Hernando County deputies to stand by. He ran outside and saw a two-ton single-axel truck with several men throwing ladders on the jail roof. "Oh hell! It's a jailbreak!" With this, ole Cecil ran back into the office to the radio and hit the mike button and said, "All Hernando County Units, 10-24, Hernando County Jail." That meant, "Help immediately." He started calling people at the top, telling them there was a jail break in progress, with people throwing ladders on the side of the jail.

When Cpt. Johnny Touchtone was contacted by Cecil, he said, "Run in the gun bunker." You've got the combination and get that Thompson out quick. I'll call the city. They're right there close. You go put them under arrest with that Thompson machine gun. The city will be there in a minute and then our deputies."

Ole Cecil ran out the door with the machine gun and a spotlight and yelled, "You're all under arrest! Get your hands up quick, or I'll blast you with this Thompson."

All the men dropped their hammers and buckets and yelled, "Don't shoot! Don't shoot! Don't shoot! Didn't anybody tell you we were going to do the roof on the old jail at night? It's too damn hot in the daytime."

Ole Cecil said, "That's a likely story. Don't move until the help gets here."

About that time, the city and three deputies slid into the front parking lot of the sheriff's office and jail, along with Cpt. Johnny Touchtone.

The men were ordered by Captain Touchtone to come down from the ladders on the side of the county jail, while the other officers held their spotlights and guns on them. The foreman had a large brush with black tar in his right hand as he approached the heavily armed officers on the ground.

He asked, "Who's in charge of you Keystone cops?"

Capt. Johnny Touchtone answered, "I am. I'm the captain."

The supervisor from the roofing company said, "Well, didn't anybody tell you, Mr. Captain, that we were coming in tonight to do the roof on the old county jail?"

Now, the captain kind of turned red in the face and said, "No. No one told me."

"Mr. Captain, can you see now we are here to patch the roof on the old county jail and not break anyone out?"

The captain replied, "Yes, I can."

The foreman of the roofing company then slapped that big tar brush into Capt. Johnny Touchtone's hand and said, "Here, Mr. Bigshot, you patch the damn roof because I think what we have hea is a failua to communicate."

With that, the men loaded their truck and drove away, leaving ole Captain Touchtone to be tarred and feathered by the high sheriff the next morning!

THE COUNTY'S FIRST BIG DRUG BUST

. . . .

Jeff was a young rookie feeling his oats one Saturday night in the summer while working the west side of Hernando County.

About eleven o'clock, Jeff was on patrol in the area of CR 595, in the Weeki Wachee. He would usually check the 7-Eleven near the old Christian camp near Weeki Wachee River. Early that day, it had rained about two inches, and once the rain cleared off, it was cool with a bright, shining full moon.

Jeff was driving around slowly, with his lights off, checking the area businesses. He knew he might be able to slip up on a bad guy in the act of a crime with his lights off.

As Jeff headed back toward the 7-Eleven, up by the Christian camp, he pulled into the store, and the store clerk gave him the thumbs-up that everything was okay; she had locked up the store.

When Jeff passed the Old Dixie Road, he glanced to the left and saw what appeared to be chrome sparkling in the bright moonlight. As he was taught, a good law enforcement officer would take a second look. Also, Jeff's curiosity told him to turn around and ease back down the Old Dixie Road. As Jeff turned onto the muddy, swampy road, he saw it sparkle again. Jeff eased along until he came upon a car parked on the right side of the muddy, swampy road, which seemed very suspicious to this young rookie. He thought about being so far out and the dangers in the swamp, with only one other officer on duty, but he knew he had a job to do.

Jeff called for a backup to the only other deputy on duty, Deputy Bill Brayton. Jeff asked him what his location was. Bill said, "About five miles east of Brooksville." He then asked Bill to head his way because he might have a drug drop on the Old Dixie Road. Jeff knew it would take Bill awhile to get there. He ran the tag number on the car, and it was registered to a subject in Pasco County. It was not reported stolen.

He was sitting in the dark to see if anyone was around. About that time, he saw a figure coming out of the swamp to his right heading toward the car. Jeff was sitting just far enough back that the subject did not see him sitting in his patrol car. He opened the patrol car door quietly and easily and stood up outside his door, knowing the dome light had been fixed so it would not come on when the door was opened. Jeff knew he had to be cautious because help was a long way off.

About that time, the subject spotted the patrol car and stopped before reaching the road. Jeff then put a spotlight on him and ordered him to freeze and to put his hands behind his head. He decided to play a hunch. Jeff then approached the subject with his eight-inch Kel-Lite in his left hand and his right hand on his .357 Magnum in his holster. Jeff had written the tag number in his left hand in case he was injured or killed so law enforcement officers would find the tag number of the car. Upon looking closer at the subject, he appeared to be a long-haired hippie dude. At this time, he knew that Deputy Bill Brayton would not be too many miles away.

Jeff asked the young fella what he was doing in the swamp in the middle of the night. The hippie said that he had to pee.

Jeff replied, "Damn, brother, why did you have to get so far out in the swamp? Ain't nobody around here for twenty miles if you were to pee on the hard road."

Jeff realized at this point his suspicions were unfolding. He then asked the hippie to turn around and walk back down to what appeared to be a trail coming out of the swamp. The hippie was reluctant but agreed to walk ahead of Jeff back down into the swamp. This young rookie realized he was moving into a dangerous situation and became even more vigilant. He unholstered the magnum and held it down to his right side as the pair walked farther into the swamp.

About forty yards off the road, they walked up on several big paper bags and two larger plastic bags, which appeared to be drugs. The young rookie told the hippie to turn around and place his hands behind his back, at which time Jeff cuffed the long-haired hippie for his own safety. Jeff knew it had rained two inches that day, but the bags were still dry. Upon closer inspection of the bags, he discovered eighteen bricks of hashish, about two thousand assorted pills in the other plastic bags, and three pounds of loose marijuana in a sack.

Jeff knew then it was time to get out of the area before another bad guy came to collect the stash. He told the subject to start walking in front of him slowly. They moved back through the swamp to the patrol car. At that point, Jeff called Bill to kick it up a notch.

Bill asked, "What you got?"

Jeff replied, "More drugs than I have ever seen."

In the early 1970s, if you got a small bag of marijuana off a subject, it was considered a good bust, but this was unbelievable to this young rookie. Jeff was excited to have such a large drug haul. He knew it would be Hernando County's largest drug haul to date.

Bill Brayton pulled up, and Jeff noticed the steam coming out from under the hood of Bill's patrol car. Jeff knew Bill had pushed hard to get to him because of the situation. When Bill saw the amount of the drugs, he said, "Man, you hit the jackpot. How do you find the kind of things you do?"

"Aggressive patrol work and always taking a second look. That is what I was taught by some of the best." They both were excited about taking the drugs off the street.

The subject was walked back to the patrol car and read his Miranda rights and asked to sign a consent to search his vehicle. Once the consent was signed, the car was searched by the deputies, who found more marijuana and paraphernalia in the vehicle. The deputies inventoried the vehicle and tagged all the evidence with a case number.

As they started back to the sheriff's office on Jefferson Street, Jeff felt the adrenaline pumping. He had played a hunch and came up with the county's first big drug haul.

Two days later, the *Hernando Press*, the local newspaper, read, "Alert young deputy played a hunch and made the county's largest single drug bust Saturday night."

A few days later, one of the county commissioners approached him at the courthouse and said, "Boy, you were lucky the other night." And then he said, "You shouldn't take so many chances like you did Saturday night."

Jeff said, "With all due respect, Mr. Commissioner, if the county would fund us enough money to hire more deputies, we wouldn't have to take such risks." He also advised the commissioner, "I work the entire county alone when the other deputy that works nights is off. It's mighty lonely out there when you have to run from one side of the county to the other side when you have a major crime, and the only backup you have is a trooper, if one is out. Or you might have to call for a backup from one of the surrounding counties, if they have any deputies out."

There were many nights in the early 1970s that Jeff would work the entire county by himself after 2:00 a.m. There were a few times, only by the grace of God, that the young rookie went home in the morning to his family.

Florida Highway Patrol Trooper, Ronald G. Smith,
Killed in the line of duty December 23, 1973, near
the Florida Barge Canal, at Red Level, Florida

OFFICER DOWN

....

This chapter is dedicated to Trooper Ronald Gordon Smith.

In 1973, I had been on the road as a patrol deputy about two years. I thought I had experienced about everything a law enforcement officer could experience. Little did I know. One quiet Sunday morning, on December 23, 1973, about eight thirty, an old friend Cliff Batten and I were standing at the front counter at the old sheriff's office on Jefferson Street in Brooksville, drinking coffee and talking to the dispatcher Ronnie.

There were two radios going and the phone for the dispatcher to take care of. Cliff and I were talking about our new patrol cars. The main radio volume was always turned up, but the intercity radio was kept low because of the amount of traffic on it from the highway patrol. While standing at the counter, I thought I heard on the intercity radio, someone on the highway patrol band said something about a trooper being "shot or shot at" just south of the Cross Florida Barge Canal in Citrus County.

"Guys, did y'all hear that?" The two men didn't hear it. I said, "Listen!"

About that time, a voice came back on again, "a Trooper has been shot and needs help north of Crystal River."

"Let's go!"

Cliff and I ran out the front door, and I jumped into my new Dodge and Cliff into his new Chevrolet. As we took off across the parking lot, all the adrenaline in the world seemed to be pumping through my body. A brother needed help. I remember thinking, *Would this new Dodge hold together at 130 mph that far?*

I switched my Motorola radio over to scan FHP. I could hear they were calling troopers out all over. As we made the Chassahowitzka curve, I had slowed to about 80 mph and looked back at Cliff in that Chevrolet; he was drafting my bumper, moving us even faster on Highway 19 North. I knew that Dodge was new and quickly glanced down at the gauges—everything was okay.

I pushed the Dodge up Highway 19 North, reaching the speed of 140 mph. The highway seemed to get narrow at this kind of speed. I glanced in the side mirror and saw two FHP troopers coming toward us. I felt my leg begin to quiver trying to hold the gas pedal on the floor.

One good thing, it was Sunday morning and almost no traffic was on Highway 19. As we sped north, it seemed so surreal to be moving in the direction of the unknown. I had never been so eager to get somewhere to help a "brother."

At this point, I did not know which trooper had been shot, but every officer within the surrounding five counties were brothers in those days, almost like family. As we got closer, I could see flashing lights at the scene at Red Level. We didn't let up until we were on the scene. I remember pulling the Dodge to the right side of Highway 19, with Cliff behind me.

I could see two or three officers standing behind a state trooper's car behind a clump of palmettos as I ran to them. We were approximately thirty or forty feet off US Highway 19 North. The trooper's car was still running. As I looked around, I could see the trooper's car door was open. I saw the trooper lying in the sandy soil just outside the car door, and I saw his pistol lying in the sand near his hand. I knew we were too late; he was already gone. As I looked down again, I recognized my friend, Ronald.

Ronald was the new trooper in Troop C, who had just graduated from the academy in Tallahassee about six months before. We would have coffee at the sheriff's office in Brookville when he would come into the office to turn his paperwork in.

Cliff and I just stood at the rear of the car as no one was saying a word. We knew not to get any closer because we did not want to disturb any evidence. We saw five hunters standing on the side of an adjoining road. We found out later they had witnessed the entire incident and came to the aide of Ronald by shooting one bad guy in the foot and then shooting a tire out on their car as they tried to escape. We later discovered the killers were from another state. The killer was an escapee, while the other a fugitive on the run.

Ron was a very quiet, friendly young man, with a gentle smile, blond hair, and blue eyes. As I turned around and looked at Cliff, I could feel the tears running down my face. I said, "Cliff, that's the new kid that moved down here a few months ago from Tallahassee." I knew I couldn't break down at this point, as we turned and walked back to our vehicles. We knew there was nothing else for us to do but go back to Hernando County. I remember turning my car around on Highway 19, as I headed south, and I could feel the tears flowing even harder. I knew I had lost a new friend.

I remember thinking to myself, *Why in the hell does anybody want to do this job?* I knew that there was nothing else we could do; I felt a deep sense of sorrow!

I found out a few days later that Ronald had moved into a new home in Crystal River after bringing his wife and little girl down. It was such a tragic thing to happen, especially, two days before Christmas.

A short time later, the governor of Florida, Rueben Askew, presented the hunters with an award for bravery and heroic actions taken on that tragic day.

Little did I know, approximately forty years later, I would meet his daughter and family at the Bridge Dedication Ceremony and Luncheon at the new bridge dedication at the Cross Florida Barge Canal in Inglis, Florida. I was greeted by two lieutenant colonels from the Florida Highway Patrol. It was a great day, and they were thankful for me trying to aide Ron. Several people took pictures of me with the colonels. I am sad to say, my dear friend, Clifford Batten, was not there to share this occasion since he had passed on.

I'm sure he and Ronald are together in heaven because old law enforcement officers never die, but they just regroup in heaven.

YANKEES AND GRITS

Now, ole Deputy Cooter Elrod shared this story with me one time, and I would like to pass it along to you.

Now, ole Cooter was somewhat known as a character. It was just in his nature, but when it came time to do his job, he was always very professional but did like to get a laugh every now and then or pull a fast one on somebody.

One morning while working the east side of the county near I-75, he was having breakfast at the Holiday Inn. Now, Cooter was a big boy, and he ate a big breakfast, usually about six eggs, half a pound of bacon with grits poured over the top of them eggs, and six or eight cathead buttermilk biscuits with coffee gravy poured over the top of all of it. It looked like a mess, but ole Cooter had learned it from his grandpappy.

Let me give you Grandpappy's recipe for coffee gravy while we are talking. Some folks called it red eye, some folks called it sawmill, some folks called it a poor man's gravy, but it was made up of bacon grease, left over from frying your bacon or your fatback in a large cast-iron skillet. You take your drippings from the fatback and pour most of it off, but a little in the bottom of the pan and then pour a cup and half of black coffee and stir with black pepper.

Now, ole Cooter Elrod would go into a restaurant and order whatever he wanted and ask for coffee gravy. Most of the time, the waitress would look at him and say, "What is coffee gravy?" Cooter would explain to the waitress, who usually said, "We don't have that, sir."

He would say, "Bring me half a cup of black coffee on the side." He would get his large order.

The waitress would usually say, "What you gonna do with that extra half cup?"

He would look up at her with a kind of a grin and pour that black coffee over the grits and eggs and start whippin' it up altogether. Usually the waitress would holler, "Y'all come over here. Look at what this man is eating."

Usually several waitresses would run over and gasp, "That's ugly!"

Now ole Cooter, being the character that he was, would say, "Lotta thangs is ugly, but they sure are good to eat." Who couldn't love ole Cooter!

He told me that one morning, a large family of Yankees came into the Holiday Inn off I-75 for breakfast and decided to sit at the table right next to him. He noticed their Bronx accent right away. They spoke Bronx heavily.

That pretty little Stephanie was the waitress that morning. She came out to the table, swishing and swooping, over to them Yankees and said, "What would y'all like this morning?" They ordered their drink, coffee, and juice for the kids—coffee for Grandma and Grandpa and coffee for Ma and Pa. Stephanie came back with the drinks and asked them if they knew what they wanted to eat.

She said, "Do you want toast or biscuits?"

They replied, "We will have toast."

The waitress then asked, "Do y'all want some patatars or grits?"

Now these Yankees ain't never heard of no grits. Grandpa said, "What the heck is a grit?"

It was all Cooter could do to keep from busting out laughing, but he held it all in and just decided to watch and listen. Stephanie said, "It's a Southern thang down here in the South."

The old fellar asked, "How do you eat a grit?"

She said, "Well, sir, most of us down hear eat them with butter and salt and pepper, but some folks from the North enjoy them with sugar and cream."

Now the whole group seemed to be fascinated about these grits. They decided to have them Southern style.

Now ole Cooter was taking all this in and was about to bust wide open a laughin'. About this time, he was finishing his breakfast, and he had a thought. Being the character that he was, he decided to pull one on the Yankees. After all, they had won the war. He figured he owed them something. As he walked by the table where the family was sitting, he said, "Good morning y'all. I hate to interrupt y'all, but I noticed that y'all are kind of took up with these grits."

They said, "We really like them, but we are very curious about how you grow them. What are they?"

Now, ole Cooter Elrod just couldn't stand it. He had to do it. He said, "Well, folks, I heard y'all say you were going to Disney World. When you leave the Holiday Inn parking lot, turn left on Highway 50 East. That will take you over into Sumter County, heading toward Disney. You'll notice several places along Highway 50. In the grit fields, the farmers are combining grits right now. If you wave a red flag or something, he'll stop his combine to see what you want, or one of the trucks in the field will come over to see if you need help. When he gets over to you, ask him if he can cut you some of that stuff and let you take some fresh grits to New York City." Cooter knew it was brown top millet, not grits. With this, they were plum delighted. Cooter said, "Y'all have a real good day. Hope y'all enjoy Disney and them grits!" Now the big guy swaggered out to his patrol car like John Wayne had captured the Comanche Tribe.

As Cooter started driving out of the parking lot, he began to think about the whole situation. It struck him like lightning. He began to think, *What will this farmer gonna say to these folks when they pull over and ask for a few handfuls of them grits on the stalk?* He began to laugh so hard he started to cry. Cooter said that he didn't know when the laughing stopped and the crying began when he realized them Yankees might call the sheriff in Hernando County and tell him in that Bronx lingo, "You've got one crazy-ass deputy" and that "he outta be fired after he pulled this on us." The sheriff knew ole Cooter meant no harm and he was one of the best deputies he had at solving crimes. He might act a little crazy sometimes, but he was a good officer.

The next two weeks went by without incident, but one morning, the sheriff called Cooter on the radio.

"70 to 11. What's your 10-20?"

"I'm up here on Norris Bishop Loop."

"10-56 me at my office, now!"

The sheriff was one of the lasts ole Southern sheriffs. He had been in office for thirty years, and everybody cut him a wide path. Now Cooter's mind began to think about all the things he might have done wrong or might have done right, but the big sheriff didn't call you to the office for nothing. That's why Cooter liked to work the midnight shift. All the brass was usually at home in bed, but you never knew in the middle of the night when you might hear, "70 to 11. What's your 10-20?" This would make you wonder why he wanted to know where you were. Ummm!

Cooter had the meeting at the sheriff's office. When he came out of the big man's office, Ronnie, the dispatcher, laughed as Cooter walked by the dispatch and said, "Hey, Cooter. What's that size thirteen cowboy boot imprint in your butt?" Cooter took his hell-raising, fist-pounding, butt-chewing and got out of town, back in the country where he belonged, talking to his friends out in the northeastern side of the county, where all was usually quiet. He would stop by some ranchers and farmers to check on the livestock to see if anything had happened on that side of the county that he loved so much.

He told me after a long career he enjoyed his retirement, sitting in his rocking chair on the front porch, thinking about the old days and all the people that he had known, like Lieutenant Bob Farrier and Trooper Tommy Greer, who was such a good young man. They would enjoy a chew under an oak tree beside the road to take a break and talk a spell. People like that and several other law enforcement officers in the area, he really loved like a brother, but the good thoughts and good times always stood out the most in his mind, even though most of them were older than Cooter and had now passed on. He remembered those times with fond memories, as he sat and petted his ole hound dog, chewing his Red Man chewing tobacco, and spitting tobacco juice in his wife's flower garden.

Every now and then, I will see ole Cooter uptown standing around the ole courthouse talking to somebody and telling one of his stories. He really enjoyed telling the story about the Yankees and the grits.

HERNANDO COUNTY MAN ENCOUNTERS CREATURE FROM ANOTHER WORLD

On March 2, 1965, the local newspaper *Hernando Sun* reported that a local man, John Reed, had called the sheriff's office to report what he claimed to be a flying saucer landing near his home, just east of the Fire Tower on Highway 50 West, now known as Cortez Boulevard, on the north side of the highway.

The story was conveyed to Deputy Jeff Duval some years later at the ole county sheriff's office on Jefferson Street in downtown Brooksville by Nelson "Red" Brass, commonly known as Red by the local people in the county. Everyone knew Red. Jeff said he had known Red since he was a young boy living in the Mountain Park area of the county, which was about two miles west of Brooksville on old Highway 50.

Jeff told me that he and Red were sitting by the fireplace on a cold, rainy night at the ole sheriff's office in about 1969. Red told Jeff he had been dispatched to meet John Reed at the scene where the spacecraft had landed. Jeff said that Red had told him that he had been shown the site by Reed. There were three or four pad marks that looked like something heavy had been pushed in the ground. At the center of these pad marks, there were signs that the sand had melted and turned into glass from some kind of heat. Red also said that Reed told him that the saucer slowly opened a door that folded downward like a ramp. Reed said at this point he became very fearful and darted back in the brush and lost his glasses. Red said Reed then told him that a small gray creature appeared in the door with a box similar to an old Polaroid camera and moved slowly down the ramp toward Reed. Reed then told Red the creature had a small gray body with a large head, a slit where the mouth should be and large dark eyes. The creature spoke no words through the slit that was similar to a mouth. Reed said he asked the creature if he would take him for a ride in the spacecraft, and the creature asked him where he would like to go, and Reed told him he would like to go around the moon and back. At this time, the creature told him he would come back and take him for a ride around the moon and back and bring him home safely.

Reed went on to tell that the creature communicated with him telepathically that he was not here to harm him. Reed said that the creature then dropped what looked like a piece of parchment paper, kind of tan in color and about the size of a legal pad, with strange markings that appeared to be in hieroglyphic script. Red also said at this time Reed gave him the parchment-looking paper with the strange markings that neither he nor Reed could decipher.

Red continued to tell Jeff that once he had the strange material in his hand, he knew he had never felt nor seen anything like it before. He told Jeff he tried to tear it, cut it, and burn it without any sign of what he had tried to do being left on the strange material.

Red then told Jeff he called the sheriff's office and told them to contact MacDill Air Force Base in Tampa. MacDill immediately dispatched a team to the site and was there in no time at all and cordoned off the area. Red said the team from MacDill took possession of the strange material with the writing. They took John Reed aside and told Red to leave the cordoned area. He obeyed their order and called the sheriff. Upon Sheriff Lowman's arrival, he was not allowed to enter the area either. Red further stated that no one was allowed in the area after MacDill authorities arrived to start their investigation.

Jeff said he then asked Red since the incident happened in 1965 if he had heard any more about what had happened to the material he recovered from Reed. Red said that he had not heard or seen anything else about the strange material and had no contact from any federal officers or MacDill Air Force Base regarding this strange encounter.

Sometime later, before 1967, Reed claimed that the spacecraft returned to the same location one afternoon as he was walking through the woods looking for snakes for his son's college project. The creature made contact again, and Reed was invited inside the ship to see the strange sights inside. There was a least one other small creature inside the spacecraft. They began to look Reed over very carefully and examined his body. They then made good on their promise, according to Reed. He said he remembered seeing the moon from the dark side, a close encounter with the surface of the moon. He further stated that time seemed nonexistent and did not really know how long they were gone but was returned safely to where the original site was. As he disembarked the spacecraft, the one creature raised his arm toward Reed as if to say goodbye.

At this point in time, John Reed said the spacecraft rose slowly for about a hundred yards and then within a matter of one or two seconds was out of sight and was never seen again by John Reed.

John Reed, a short time later, began building a model of the spacecraft, just east of the old Fire Tower on Highway 50 West. It was a scale model of the spacecraft that Reed claims he saw and rode in. The model sat approximately fifty yards north of Highway 50, or Cortez Boulevard, on display for many years.

People from all over the country and all around the world came to photograph John Reed and his flying saucer. He was known as the "Flying Saucer Man" to the local people.

This story was told to Jeff Duval by Nelson "Red" Brass, deputy sheriff of Hernando County, who he had known for many years and who he had worked with. Nelson "Red" Brass retired after twenty years of service and lived on his ranch, out in the Annutteliga Hammock. Jeff was very privileged to have worked with Red Brass on his ranch occasionally along with his son-in-law, Danny Spencer, and Doug Chorvat and the ole country preacher, Brother Dave Stephens.

Jeff just had to mention Red Brass's buckskin cattle horse. Jeff said he watched that horse work, and no cow or steer could stay in front of him. Red asked Jeff one day, "Do you want to ride him to see what a real cowboy's horse is like?" Jeff told him sure. Jeff got in the saddle, and they turned a steer loose, and that eight-hundred-pound horse knew exactly every move it made at the moment Jeff made it, and all he had to do was hang on and stay in the saddle. That buckskin was the most amazing horse Jeff had ever seen working cattle.

Red was the first hired deputy sheriff in Hernando County, as Sheriff Lowman worked the county by himself from 1949 until Red Brass was hired in the early 1950s to assist him. Red was a true Florida cracker cowboy, and it was an honor and a pleasure to have worked with him in law enforcement and on horseback. He joined the Hernando County Sheriff's Posse in 1972, after the posse was formed by Deputy Jeff Duval.

POSSE

Jeff was working in the office of Sheriff Sim L. Lowman. Now ole Sim was a hard-nosed, old-school, cracker sheriff. He took office in 1949 and was sheriff for thirty years until he retired.

Jeff's mind was wondering one night while working a twelve-hour shift in the office. Jeff got to thinking, *Sometimes the department needs extra help*. He was thinking about a group of men on horseback, because they could go where a man could not, and that surely might be helpful sometimes on manhunts or responding to someone lost in the woods. However, he was somewhat apprehensive about talking to the Big Man.

A few days later, he saw the high sheriff pull up in front of the office. When the sheriff came in, Jeff approached him, since they were alone, and asked him what he would think about letting him form a group for search and rescue or a posse. The sheriff didn't seem too excited about the idea but said, "Go ahead and see what you can do with it," though Jeff knew that the sheriff had no idea what he had in mind.

The next evening when he came to work, he started making phone calls to local cowboys, ranchers, businessmen, and a few longtime friends. Jeff was the kind of fella that when he got something in his mind, he would go wide open until he got something accomplished.

Within three weeks, Jeff had the first meeting at the sheriff's office one evening about seven o'clock. Approximately twenty men from Hernando County showed up for the meeting. Jeff had also contacted one of the majors from the Hillsborough County Sheriff's

Office in Tampa, who was eager to help Jeff form a posse, or whatever they could do to help Hernando County get started.

One of the first issues for the group was to earn money and set up a rank and file for the next meeting. It was Jeff's intention for this to be a civic organization, set up to aid the sheriff's office at the sheriff's discretion.

About a month later, they had another meeting to elect officers for the newly formed group "the Hernando County Sheriff Mounted Posse." Almost all the men knew Jeff and elected him president.

Since it was a civic organization, not dependent on tax dollars, they had to raise their own money for uniforms, horse blankets, and flags. The blankets for the horses were green with gold trim, HCSO, and a sheriff's star on the right front. The men's uniforms were basically the same as the deputies, except for the patch. They looked sharp once all the equipment came in.

The posse would meet once a month at the sheriff's office on Jefferson Street for special training. They all had been appointed special deputy status. They could not wear a weapon since they were not bonded.

At the time the posse was founded, Jeff did not own a horse. An old friend rancher, Monroe, who had known Jeff for many years would loan Jeff a horse whenever they were out in the field until Jeff could find him a horse, which he did later. It was a beautiful golden palomino stud, El Jose, a little wiry, but Jeff loved the horse.

It wasn't long before the posse was invited to be in the Brooksville Christmas Parade. They looked sharp with all the tack and gear, flags, and uniforms. They took first place in the Christmas parade that year. They always rode in formation wherever they went. The sheriff was very happy and so were all the members of the posse. Jeff had his regular deputy patrol duties as well as running the posse. Jeff loved every minute of it, and the members worked well together.

One Friday morning, the sheriff was contacted by the Citrus County Sheriff's Office. They were requesting help in the search of a nine-year-old girl that had gone missing Friday afternoon after getting off her school bus near Crystal River. The posse was sent into the Chassahowitzka Swamp to search the area off Highway 19, since

Citrus County was searching north. The chief deputy, a longtime rancher and cowboy, was leading them through the swampy area. They came out of the swamp about sunset.

The next day, the posse was sent north of the swamp, up Highway 19, for another all-day search with nothing found. That afternoon as they came out and were riding back to the trailers in single file, Jeff was riding close behind Monroe. The posse was all worn-out. Suddenly, Monroe's mare horse jumped and kicked Jeff in the left shin bone. Man, it sounded like someone had hit a home run!

Jeff rolled off his horse onto the ground yelling, "My leg is broke!"

Ole Monroe just laughed and said, "You ought to know not to ride that gelding up too close to this ole gal."

Jeff was still rolling around on the ground moaning in agony and holding his leg. He said, "I think my damn leg is broke, Monroe!" Jeff knew he was riding with a tough bunch of Florida cowboys. One of the men came riding back and helped him up, but Jeff knew he had to be as tough as the rest. He didn't want the men to think that he was any less tough than they were. With some help, Jeff grabbed the saddle horn, swung his leg on over the horse, and rode on in. That evening when Jeff got home, his wife helped him pull his boots off. His leg was swollen, and there was blood in the boot, but he had "cowboyed up" one more time.

The posse was sent back the next day to aid in the search for the little girl. Unfortunately, she was not found until about a week later by using dogs from the state prison system.

The investigation revealed that when she got off the school bus, a man laying cable saw her getting off the bus on the lonely road. As she walked by the man, he stopped her and started a conversation with her and then grabbed the child, shoved her into the cable van, and took her to a remote wooded area. He then raped the child and then strangled her with a wire cord and then dragged her farther into the woods and left her lifeless body there like she was nothing.

The Citrus County Sheriff's Investigators led by Sheriff B. R. Quinn didn't stop. They backtracked the day the young girl got off the bus and found that the cable repairman was the only person in the area when the child got off the school bus. When they picked him up and interviewed him, he later confessed to the crime and was sentenced to death.

Sheriff Sim L. Lowman later told the posse members he was proud of them for their part in helping Citrus County in the case. Jeff also told the men he was also proud of them and that they had done a good job.

After all, the Chassahowitzka swamp is a very dangerous place. There were times the men had to lead the horses in chest-deep water and mud, full of alligators and snakes!

Jeff said that at the end of the day, he became separated from his chief deputy, Red Brass, and had to really cowboy up to keep his mind from thinking about spending the night in the swamp. However, just about dusk, he saw a clearing and found his way to the main road and to the staging area.

Several days later, the Citrus County Sheriff's Office notified Sheriff Lowman the nine-year-old girl's body was recovered. The assailant was sentenced to death. This story is dedicated to the memory of her.

NOW TALKING ABOUT COWBOYING UP

Now, talking about cowboying up, it ain't easy sometimes.

One afternoon, Jeff was out at his place on Highway 491. He had bought a beautiful bay mare quarter horse, about 1,100 pounds of green-broke horse flesh. He had decided, after having her for about three months—grooming, feeding, and playing with the big girl—that it was time for them to get more acquainted. About four o'clock in the afternoon on Saturday, he told his wife, "Let's go out to the pasture. Bring some feed. I'm going to ride that mare."

Bobbie said, "Jeff, that is a mighty big horse. You be careful. She is green."

With that, he grabbed the tack, she got the feed and the boys, and they followed him out to the pasture.

Little Jeff said, "Daddy, are you really going to ride that horse?"

With that, he smiled. The boys and their mama were going to see a show, but Jeff didn't realize it at the time. He put his foot in the stirrup and eased up into the saddle. The big girl took about three steps forward and then went wild, bucking, jumping, and spinning around. In about five seconds, Jeff's butt hit the old hammock ground hard. He grabbed the reins.

Bobbie and the boys were laughing. She said, "You can't ride that horse."

He replied, "There ain't no horse that I can't ride."

He put his foot back in the stirrup and mounted the horse again, and this time, he stayed on about six seconds and then hit the ground with a loud thud! This time, there was no laughing. He knew not to stick those cowboy boots too far into the stirrups with a horse like this. A big horse like this could drag you to death before she stopped running, but he knew the old cowboy sayin', "You gotta cowboy up!"

The sixth time his body hit the ground, he was hurtin' all over.

Bobbie asked, "Honey, how many times are you going to get back on that horse?"

He answered, "I think one more time."

As he limped back over and took the reins, it took all that he could do to pull himself back up into the saddle the seventh time. When he hit the ground this time, he didn't get up. Bobbie and the boys came running out into the pasture and helped him get up. As she helped him limp back to the house, little Jeff led the horse back to the stall.

Bobbie asked, "Do you think anything is broken?"

He replied, "I am not sure. Help me get into the shower, and I will lay down for a while."

His boys unsaddled the horse along with their mom. When they came back into the house, Jeff was lying on the bed, after getting his dirty clothes off and taking a shower. They all three walked up to the bedside, and Bobbie asked, "Do you want to go to the hospital?"

He said, "I will let you know in the morning."

As he looked up at his family, little Jeff said, "Daddy, you done good!"

A few days later, he decided to sell the horse after finding out the horse had been abused by another man when it was younger. That's why a man could never ride this horse. A few days later, a young girl from Citrus County bought the horse and won several ribbons in barrel racing and roping. He was happy he had found the horse a good home, but he will never forget the day he decided to ride that big mare. He had to show himself he was as tough as anyone around, but in his older years, he paid his dues; being tough isn't what it's made out to be. Knowing when to quit is an asset, and it can cause you a whole lot less pain in your old age!

Deputy Jeff Duval's Adored Horse "El Jose"

HIPPIES GET DOWN

. . . .

Jeff and I were talking one night, and he told me how law enforcement was different in 1972 and how back in the day things were wild and wooly.

He told me a story about an arrest he had made. He said around two o'clock one morning, while working his twelve-hour shift, he was out cruising the county in the full moon and drove into the old Story Rock Mine to poke around looking for anything out of the ordinary in the moonlight. He said he parked his patrol car and got out to take a "wiz"! Suddenly, he said he looked down in the abandoned rock pit and saw the walls in the huge open pit flashing psychedelic disco colors. He said his face lit up as well. He said to himself, *Dang, it's a hippy party and I'm inviting myself!*

Jeff said he walked up to the edge of the big pit and saw what looked like a huge wild party of "Wild West Indians" dancing around a fire. He said he was thinking, *Boy, howdy, I'm gonna enjoy this.*

Jeff said he called for the only other deputies working that night, Bill Brayton and old cracker Deputy Nig Mills, to assist him in rounding up the tribe of long-haired hippies.

Jeff said he just sat back and enjoyed the show until the other deputies arrived. Bill brought a K-9 named Smokey, a black shepherd dog, to help in the capture of this bunch of long hairs. Now, Smokey spent his entire adult life as a deputy sheriff. He was a good dog in his day. At the end, Smokey was retired and spent his remaining days with his last handler, Bruce.

Jeff said he had a plan to walk down the pit road in the dark and slip in on the pit full of hippies. The plan worked. When they saw ole Smokey, he alerted and began to bark. They were told to hold their hands up, to stand still, and to turn off the hippy music, to which they complied.

Jeff said he told them, "Y'all under arrest!"

He said one wild child spoke up, "For what?"

Ole Jeff told them in a joking manner, "For having too much fun in this county, and I'm sure for possessing drugs and trespassing too." Jeff said when they lined the group up to walk them out, there were twenty-seven boys and two girls. "Hum, can you imagine!"

When the parade arrived at the county jail, the hippy boys were lined up out the front door and down the street for half a block. It was a record for the largest single arrest at one time and still stands to this day.

The owner of the mine pit gave orders to arrest anyone for trespassing because a young fella was killed the month before diving off the pit wall. It rectified the problem.

It just goes to show you what a deputy sheriff can run into in the quiet hours of the night using good patrol tactics and looking for out-of-the-way things and being alert, kind of like the night Jeff and Deputy Leander Lawson took a trip through the Croom Game Reserve and found a casket sitting in the middle of Trail 22. "Huh, makes you wonder!"

What kind of freaks and weirdos would take a body out of a coffin and leave it sitting in the middle of the game reserve road? Oh well, there are more freaks and weirdos to come along as his career moved along.

DEATH AND DANGERS ON THE ROAD

Jeff and I were sitting around the campfire one night during huntin' season up in Gulf Hammock. We were telling stories about things we would never forget. He began to share a story about five hunters that had been out all day, drinking and riding around in a jeep somewhere around Richloom on the east side of Hernando County.

He said he was working the midnight shift, and around two thirty on a Sunday morning, he was dispatched to the Lighthouse Bar on Highway 301 South of Ridge Manor, Florida, in reference to five men with shotguns shooting up the place. In the 1970s in Hernando County after 2:00 a.m., you only had one deputy out to cover the whole county. He knew of the Lighthouse to be a rough spot and knew the only help he might get would be out of one of the surrounding counties or the Florida Highway Patrol.

At the time he was dispatched, he was on Mondon Hill Road, approximately two miles south of Highway 50. He contacted dispatch in Brooksville by radio and advised them he was 10-51, 10-18, which meant in route at a high rate of speed with lights and siren. He asked dispatch if he could round up someone from the surrounding counties to head his way but came up short with no help.

About this time, dispatch in Brooksville advised that more shots had been fired inside the bar and there were five men armed with twelve-gauge shotguns shooting up the bar. He further stated that it was calls like these that made your hair stand up on the back of your neck because you knew you were alone to handle a situation more than likely by yourself and he knew he had taken an oath to uphold the law no matter what. On the way to the call, he remembered what ole Deputy Red Brass once told him—situations like this, you can do one of two things, take the badge off and go home or do your sworn duty and possibly be killed. I knew Jeff was not the kind of man to back up.

He told me when he arrived, the five drunks were coming out of the Lighthouse Bar holding shotguns. Just as he was pulling off Highway 301, into the parking lot, one of the drunk hunters fired a shot, shooting a parking lot light out. Jeff slid to a stop at the edge of Highway 301 in the parking lot to see if they were going to shot at him. They did not but lowered their guns and got into the jeep. Jeff said he knew there was no one coming to help him. He did what he was sworn to do. He eased into the parking lot up near the jeep sideways, got out of his patrol car, and stood behind the door after turning the lights and siren off.

He said it was times like this when you must be very cool and levelheaded if you want to live another day. He said he yelled at the guys in the jeep, "Hey, guys, looks like you're having a hell of a good time." The drunk that shot the light out in the parking lot was sitting in the back of the jeep holding his shotgun straight up. He said he had heard other law enforcement officers say they were never scared. Jeff told me he believed that was a damn lie or the man was a fool, because he was plenty scared. He knew he had to go easy.

The guy in the back seat, said, "We're having one hell of a good time tonight. What's the problem?"

He replied, "Can I ease up there and talk to you, boys, man-to-man?"

One of the other fellas said, "Yeah, come on up here."

Jeff eased forward, still positioning the car between him and the shooters. He stepped out and said, "Guys, nothing wrong with having a good time. I've done it myself. The only problem tonight, y'all have caused quite a bit of property damage."

Now he knew he would not take these guys to jail himself without winning them over with some quick-thinking and slow-talking, low-key stuff psychology. If it didn't work, he knew what the results would be.

He said at this time, "Boys, you can do one of two things: unload those guns and turn them over to me or you can kill me, but there is about twenty people on the way that will be here shortly." He knew full well that wasn't true, but he was sure praying it worked.

The drunk that shot the light out said, "Screw you! We ain't going nowhere with you."

His reply was, "Look, no one has been hurt tonight, yet think about that. I'm willing to let y'all go home after I issue all of you a summons to appear in court and possibly get your guns back. Everyone will walk away from here tonight. No more damage done." Jeff said he knew that was the only option he had to stay alive.

The driver of the jeep spoke up and laid his shotgun on the hood since there was no top. He just laid it over the windshield and stood up and said, "Guys, he seems like a pretty good ole boy. I don't want to go to jail, and we sure as hell ain't gonna shoot him. I ain't going to the electric chair for none of you guys."

Jeff said at this point the rest of the drunks agreed to take his offer. He was standing behind the patrol car door. Jeff told them to step out of the jeep one at a time with a shotgun over the head and to slowly lower it after turning their back to him and then walk backward with the shotguns up, and Jeff took them one at a time. Once he had all the guns in the back of the patrol car and patted each one down, he wrote each one of them a summons to appear before the county judge.

The Pasco County Line was only a couple of miles south. Jeff said, "I'm going to go inside and if y'all are gone home when I come out of the bar, that would be good." Jeff went inside to talk to the owner and see the damage, which amounted to approximately $1,500.

Max, the bar owner, knew Jeff from being there on other calls, like the night he was dispatched to the bar on a call, and when he got inside the bar, he saw a man sitting on a barstool holding his guts in his hands!

Max said, "I don't know how in the world you pulled that off without getting killed."

He replied, "Well, Max, you either take the call and do your job or you take the badge off and go home. The night is still young. I'm on till six o'clock in the morning, and I pray to God I get to go home."

Jeff said that he knew that the east side of the county was a very dangerous place to work simply because it was so far away from Brooksville, Dade City, or Bushnell; and he remembered telling the sheriff, "We need more help on the east side of the county, especially four o'clock to midnight."

When you have trouble over there, it's usually at night, and it is usually bad. The sheriff's reply was "The county commission will not fund us any more money for deputies."

He said he remembered thinking, *I told y'all it's going to happen one day. I know it in my heart and in my mind.*

A few years later, Jeff made night shift commander under Sheriff Melvin Kelly, after he was elected to the position of Hernando County Sheriff. Times were beginning to change. The county was growing very rapidly on the west side.

After taking office, Sheriff Kelly started setting up a rank structure and dividing the county into three zones, the west side being Zone 1, because it was more populated, which Jeff disagreed with because Brooksville was the county seat and should have been Zone 1. That was just his thinking, but he wasn't the sheriff. Zone 2 was Brooksville area. Zone 3 was from Spring Lake east and north and south to the Sumter County Line and Pasco County Line.

In February 1978, he was a sergeant over at the East Side Substation. He had worked the day shift in February 21. It was a routine day, but it was very cold. That evening, his night deputy was Lonnie C. Colburn, a young rookie who Jeff had grown up with. "He was like a little brother to me," he said. Lonnie called him on the radio about 6:00 p.m. and said, "Sarge, I will be a little late coming over there." Jeff said he told him it would be okay and that he would wait at the Spring Lake Road. He knew Lonnie needed to gas up his patrol car and bring him some paperwork from the sheriff's office in

Brooksville to the substation. He was waiting at the intersection of Highway 50 and Mondon Hill Road. Jeff heard the radio, "No. 16 Brooksville, I'm 10-8, 10-51 to Zone 3." Jeff had no way of knowing that it would be the last time he would hear no. 16 ever again.

He called Lonnie on the radio and advised him that he was on his way home and that if he needed anything to call him. He would be there shortly. About 6:30 p.m., Jeff arrived at home, took a shower, and was beginning to relax for the evening when he heard sirens wailing in the distance, lots of sirens. He knew something was up. The phone rang, and the dispatcher advised, "Lonnie has been shot across from the substation at the Circle K." These were the most dreaded words you could ever hear.

He jumped into a pair of blue jeans, house slippers, and a T-shirt, grabbed his gun belt, and ran out the door, speeding to the scene. He arrived on the scene shortly after 7:30 p.m. and saw Lonnie's car behind the Circle K, at Highway 301 and Highway 50, with the door open and the motor running, with Nig Mills standing behind Lonnie's car crying in his hands.

Jeff jumped out of his patrol car and said, "What in the hell has happened, Nig?"

He replied, "They shot Lonnie."

The ambulance was pulling out as he was pulling in, and he could see lots of blood on the ground. He said, "Did Lonnie say anything before they put him in the ambulance?"

Nig replied, "He kept trying to get up but was bleeding very badly from the inside of his chest."

Jeff asked, "Did he have a vest on?"

Nig said, "Yes, but they shot him between the slats in the vest with his own gun."

Nig Mills was a veteran, hard-core, ole Southern deputy, hard as a case of railroad spikes. He wasn't the kind of man to cry.

About 8:00 p.m., Ernie Chatman Sr. called the substation wanting to know if it was Jeff who had been shot. They advised him they couldn't give out any information except that he was okay and out on the road. Ernie drove to Ridge Manor and met Jeff and rode with him all night. Ernie Sr. was a member of the Hernando County

Sheriff's Posse and had helped raise Jeff from the age of fourteen. Jeff was so glad to have him with him that night.

About nine o'clock that night, there were at least five hundred fellow officers from the surrounding counties at the scene assisting in combing the area for the suspects with helicopters and dogs. It was a very cold, frigid night and was very noisy at the scene with so many radios blaring and helicopters flying over.

Hernando County sheriff, Melvin Kelly, came on the radio and said, "Hernando 1 to all units, no. 16 is signal 7," which meant, "Lonnie C. Colburn is dead." He advised all Hernando County Units to meet him at the scene. When Sheriff Kelly got to the scene, he called all his deputies at the scene into a huddle around him and gave them his instructions, which I will carry to my grave. Unfortunately, Lonnie made a rookie mistake that cost him his life.

That night, Jeff said he remembered thinking, *I told y'all it's going to happen one day. I knew it in my heart and in my mind.* Years later after being disabled and beaten by a drug dealer in Gulf County and spending several weeks in the hospital in Panama City, Jeff returned to Hernando County that had been his home growing up.

In 2012, retired lieutenant Jeff Duval was interviewed at his home in Brooksville by WTVT investigative reporter Doug Smith out of Tampa on *Cop Killers*. As he conveyed the story to Doug Smith, he was asked about the two killers. He said, "They were given the death sentence thirty-eight years ago but still had not been executed after killing three young people and raping a young woman that night."

The two killers had kidnapped a young eighteen-year-old mother-to-be at gunpoint in Leesburg, Florida, earlier in the afternoon from a grocery store parking lot. She was eight months pregnant. They took her to a secluded wooded area several miles away, raped her, put her on her knees, and executed her, leaving the lifeless body of the young girl in the woods.

Jeff saw no justice in this case after thirty-eight years. He wrote the governor, Charlie Crist, a letter stating all the facts and asked him why the sentence hadn't been carried out. He never received a response from Gov. Charlie Crist, but the two killers were later commuted to life. There would be no justice served for the three victims in this case.

Jeff said he lays awake many nights with nightmares that haunt him of the things he had seen and the friends that he had lost in the line of duty.

TIME FOR A CHANGE

In Hernando County in the mid-1970s, change was slow to come to the South and the sheriff's office.

Two of the first black deputies were very good officers, Lee Andrew Lawson and Willie Brooks, and they had served honorably since the early 1960s. Hernando County took on its third and only black deputy sheriff, Floyd Moore. He had just finished his basic training and was given a blue line certification as required by the State of Florida. At this time, Floyd was assigned to Sgt. Jeff Duval to finish up the required training. Jeff was to accompany him on all calls they received and assist and further train him to be cut loose on his own.

Now Floyd Moore was a very large man, six feet, five inches, and weighed about 240 pounds. He was a very timid, quiet individual and had a good heart.

One late evening, the two men were on patrol duty. It was a quiet Sunday night. Floyd began telling the sergeant about his childhood raising. He said that his mama worked at the Lewis plantation, just south of Brooksville, cleaning cabins and taking in ironing and washing for folks in town to make ends meet. She was trying to raise two little sons on her own.

Floyd went on to tell a story about how his mama had bought their first radio and how she had forbidden them to touch it at all, but curiosity got the best of the two little fellas. One morning after their mama left to go to work, the two little fellas could not believe the voices coming out of this little box called a radio. Floyd's older brother had said they should try to get the little people out from behind the cloth on the front of that box. At which time, they went to work on the cloth speaker, not knowing what it was or where the little people in the radio were coming from. They pondered some ideas and finally decided to burn a hole in the cloth as to see who was in the box. At this age, you could understand two little boys being curious, but now they had to figure out how to get the fire out. A little water would do the job, they thought. As they looked with amazement into the dark hole, they could not find anyone doing the talking.

Floyd said his older brother became worried and realized their mama was not going to be happy with that burned hole in her new radio. It was time to get scared because their mama would be home shortly. When she got home, she severely scolded the two little fellas and scared them nearly to death but did not whip them as she was a sweet-loving mama.

Their mama worked so hard to see that the two brothers were raised right, and she wanted to make sure they had a good education. She accomplished her mission as time went on.

The sergeant and the recruit laughed about the radio story as they drove along in the cool night air. They were driving south on US 41, when Sergeant Duval told Floyd, "Now pay attention. We are going to start doing building security checks along the major highways." They pulled into a local hardware store about five miles south of Brooksville. As they pulled into the driveway, the sergeant advised Floyd to take his spotlight and look around the front of the building to see if it was secure. Floyd did just that.

Then Jeff asked, "Floyd, do you think this is sufficient on a building security check?"

Floyd answered, "Yes, sir!"

As a training officer, Jeff knew it was not. He advised Floyd, "Take your flashlight. Be careful and walk around the building and check the doors and windows in the back. Then you are completely sure that the building is secured. This is the proper way to do a business check. You might want to leave your card so the owner will know in the morning that you were here at a certain time in the middle of the night and that you are on the job."

Floyd thanked Jeff for the card idea and said, "You're right, Sergeant. Now we know for sure."

The two deputies continued their security checks throughout the night between calls.

During this time, progress was slow-coming to the south. The sheriff's office had grown from seven deputies to about twenty-five, and the officers were still working fifty to sixty hours per week, sometimes more. The west side was booming along the Gulf of Mexico. The Northerners had kept moving into the county. We now had about 35,000 people in Hernando County. It was the fastest-growing county in the State of Florida for a time. It had grown rapidly from the late 1960s. There were only about 10,000–12,000 people at that time.

The last ole Southern sheriff's ways were hard to die. Floyd was only allowed to work the black side of town. The county in some ways was still segregated.

Jeff remembered one Saturday evening they were busy. They had calls backed up, and he knew this was not good. Jeff knew the people of the county deserved better service, but they were not given the funding to hire more deputies and the sheriff would always have to go to Tallahassee to try and get more money for the sheriff's office because of the rapid growth. They were unable to keep up with the necessities that were required to do the job right.

The next weekend was a full moon, and they always seemed to get busier when the moon was full. The creatures came out to play! They were backed up on their calls as usual. Jeff called Floyd Moore on the radio and advised him to meet him at the Winn-Dixie parking lot south of Brooksville. The sergeant was sitting in his patrol car in the Winn-Dixie parking lot when Floyd pulled up. The sergeant got out of his car and was standing beside it. He asked Deputy Floyd Moore to step out because he needed to talk to him.

When Floyd got out and walked up to the sergeant, Jeff looked up at the big man that he had trained and said, "Floyd, I think it's time that we change some things around here. We are so busy I don't have time to ask permission, so I'm going to make a decision. That's why they gave me these stripes."

Floyd said, "What you need, Sergeant?"

Jeff advised Floyd he wanted him to take a call out of his normal patrol area on the south side of town, which was predominately black citizens.

Floyd Moore asked, "Are you sure I can do that?"

Jeff replied, "Walk a little closer to me. Look at my badge. What does it say?"

Floyd began reading the badge on the sergeant's chest. He said, "Deputy Sheriff, Hernando County, Florida."

The sergeant replied, "That is exactly right, Floyd. You are a deputy sheriff just like me. You have the authority, and I am giving you an order. Take the next call that comes up no matter where it is."

Floyd looked astonished but said, "Yes, sir!"

While they were standing there in the parking lot, a call came in from the Garden Grove area, approximately four or five miles south of Brooksville. Jeff said, "There's your call. Go get it." Then, he advised dispatch that Unit 17, Floyd Moore, would take the call.

Dispatch called the sergeant back and replied, "Are you sure of that, Sergeant?"

He said, "Yes, I'm sure. I advised him to take the next call. If any heat comes down on anyone, this is my decision. I will take the heat."

The call was answered by the first black deputy, to take a call out of south Brooksville.

On Monday afternoon, Sgt. Jeff Duval was called into the sheriff's office. At which time, dispatch advised, "The sheriff wants to see you in his office."

Melvin Kelly was an old friend, but Jeff knew he was the sheriff. Jeff knocked on the door, and the sheriff said, "Come on in and have a seat." The sheriff looked at Jeff with that Irish look and said, "I understand you sent Floyd Moore on a call Saturday night in Garden Grove."

Jeff replied, "Yes, sir, I did. We had several calls backed up, and he was sitting in south Brooksville not doing anything. I didn't think it would look good for you and this department to keep getting backed up on calls. You gave me these stripes because you have confidence in me. I had to make a decision. I didn't have time to ask questions, and I think you will agree, Sheriff, it's time for a change."

The sheriff leaned back in his big green office chair and said, "Maybe you are right. Nothing ever stays the same."

Jeff stood up, and the sheriff shook his hand and gave him that grin. Jeff turned to walk out, realizing this was a history-changing moment in Hernando County.

Deputy Floyd Moore continued to work until his retirement and was a very successful law enforcement officer. Jeff and Floyd remain friends to this day.

About forty years later, Jeff drove to the Winn-Dixie—the same store where he advised Deputy Moore to take that call—and saw Floyd Moore standing in the parking lot talking to some people. As Jeff walked up to say hello, he noticed the gray hair that Floyd Moore had earned, just like himself.

Floyd was telling the people, "This is my old supervisor. He taught me a lot when I was a young deputy sheriff. I took his advice in those days, and it paid off." He was telling the people the story of his first building check that Jeff had advised him on many years earlier.

"I remember one time I got a letter in my file. The sheriff called me into his office. I was worried on what I might have done wrong, but when I walked into the sheriff's office, to my amazement, the sheriff was smiling and reached to shake my hand."

As the two men shook hands, Floyd Moore said, "Sheriff, have I done something wrong?"

Sheriff Melvin Kelly smiled. "No, you did something very right. I got a letter from a businessman in the county, stating you were doing a good job. He found your card where you had checked his business at three o'clock in the morning."

They both smiled. Floyd said, "Sheriff, do you know who taught me that?"

He said, "No, who?"

Floyd answered, "Jeff Duval, when he was my sergeant."

Sheriff Kelly replied, "Job well done. You have your first good letter in your file."

The people that Floyd was talking to were amazed at the story he was telling them.

Jeff said, "Well, I got to go. It was good to see you, Floyd, and you folks too," and walked into the store. Every now and then, the path of the two old deputies will cross in town, and they will talk about the old times when they changed history in a small southern county in Central Florida.

*****

In August of 2020, I decided to look up my old friend, Floyd. I knew that age was knocking on my door and his. I didn't know when I would see him again, if I didn't go now. Saturday, I traveled to Brooksville and drove to Floyd's home in south Brooksville. I was met on the front patio by his wife of many years. She remembered me.

I said, "Where is my old friend and brother? I've missed him. I thought I better come check on him."

His wife said she would go into the house and get Floyd in just a moment. She added, "Floyd has dementia. He might not know you."

Hearing her words made my heart very sad. When she returned holding the big man's arm, I could see all seventy-seven years. His hair was white, and the age was in his eyes. I remembered he told me once that he was seven years older than me.

As I approached the patio, he looked at me straight in the eyes as if he was trying to say, "I know you." So, I took a step back, and I gave him a salute and said, "Floyd, it's your old sergeant, Jeff Duval." At this time, I knew that he remembered who I was. I saw the river of tears running down his face as he remembered all the times we had spent together, through the good and bad. He always had my back and I always had his.

HEAD NURSE

Deputy Billy Donn had a sweet tooth for the pretty gals. Now, ole Billy Donn seemed to have something about him that a lot of women were drawn to. Some said he was a lady's man.

Anyway, one day, he met a new nurse while working a case that took him into the emergency room at the old county hospital around Valentine's Day. This little nurse was quite cute. She was about twenty years old but looked much younger. Billy Donn asked for the ER nurse and someone said, "She's in number 3. Just walk in behind the curtain." He did and saw a pretty little nurse in her pressed uniform.

Billy Donn said, "Excuse me, ma'am. Are you the nurse in charge?"

She gave ole Billy Donn a sweet smile when she looked up at him, looking straight into his eyes. They looked into each other's eyes for a few seconds. "My name is Donna Bowling," she replied. And without hesitation, she said, "Did you bring me a Valentine?"

Billy Donn replied, "No, I brought you a Valentine kiss!"

Long story short, Billy Donn and the nurse were married about one year later.

One morning, about two o'clock, he came home holding a bloody bag filled with newspaper and told his wife it was a murder victim's head. The entire thing was wrapped with clear plastic.

Billy Donn told his wife not to open the refrigerator the next morning. "I must maintain the chain of evidence until I can get the victim's head to the morgue in the morning."

His wife said, "There is a dead man's head in my refrigerator, in our kitchen?"

Ole Billy Donn almost started laughing, but he had a poker face when it came to playing a joke. After all, she was a tough little nurse, he thought! She was not happy, to say the least.

The next morning, Bill Donn was awakened by her screaming, "Get this damn head out of this house right now!" He jumped up running into the kitchen. "Little Bit" was holding the refrigerator door open and was pointing at the bloody man's head all wrapped up in a plastic bag full of newspaper. He had arranged the black part to look like a beard and the red part to look like a round head.

Ole Billy Donn broke down laughing, but Nurse Little Bit did not laugh. He said, "You ain't so tough, are you?" She was almost in tears. Billy Donn gave her a reassuring hug and said, "Honey, that's only a bag of mullet!"

Laughing together, Billy Donn asked, "Sugar, can you cook this ole boy's head tonight with some grits and hush puppies?"

She gave him that female "gaze," stomped her little foot, and left him holding the bag!

SHOOTIN' BISCUIT HOLES IN THE JAILHOUSE WALL

....

The old sheriff's office was built back in the 1800s. It was a three-story wood structure building with an ole Southern colonial look, with a large front porch with pillars and a picket fence rail, lots of large windows, and a half-circle driveway in the front. The sheriff didn't mind telling anyone, "That's my parking spot," as I had learned the hard way. I remember a state trooper had parked in that spot out front. When the sheriff walked in, he said, "That's my parking spot. If you don't move that car, I'll have it towed off in five minutes." The trooper started out the door, mumbling something under his breath, he knew the sheriff well.

Now on to the biscuit holes.

One day, I was filling in on radio duty, working our usual twelve-hour shift. I had just bought my first new handgun—a shiny, nickel-plated, .38 Smith & Wesson with pearl grips. It was a nice gun. My relief was a small-framed man, who would remind you of Barney Fife. He was a great guy. He walked in about five fifteen in the afternoon that day. We went over the day's activity log. When we got through, he said, "Jeff, let me see your new gun." About that time, two big guys came in the front door. One wanted to register as a felon. I asked them to wait on the front porch while we finished up our necessary business so I could be relieved.

During this time, I had pulled my new pistol out of the drawer. Ronnie was standing at the front counter, and when I laid the gun down, his eyes lit up. "Boy, that's a beauty, Jeff. How does it feel?" he asked while picking it up. Ronnie had it pointed at the newly painted wall across from the counter. Now, I'm thinking, *He knows I didn't unload this gun, right?* Then the unbelievable happened. *Boom!* That new Smith & Wesson sounded like Dirty Harry's .44 Magnum! The bullet was ricocheting all around us making me duck and dodge as it finally hit the fireplace behind us. I looked at him in fright, not saying anything at first. He looked like Barney, who had just fired his first bullet! He was white as paper, and his eyes were as round as silver dollars.

He exclaimed, "I didn't know it was loaded!"

I replied, "What the hell would I want with an empty gun?"

About this time, one of the men on the porch cracked the door open and said, "Hey, when you two finish shooting at each other, we'll come back in." I told the guy to wait a few minutes. He closed the door not saying another word.

Still shaky, I said, "Ronnie, look at that gigantic bullet hole."

He looked at me with a ghostly look and said, "Yeah, and that wall was just painted two weeks ago!"

The wall was light green in color but was made of plaster, which made the hole look even bigger.

I told him, "Let's deal with these guys on the porch and get them out of here!" I then opened the door and said in a joking kinda way, "Come on in, men. The shootin' is over."

We quickly finished our business with the two men. As the two men walked out, one stopped and said, "You boys be careful now." I'm thinking, *Yeah, you're a smart aleck*, as they walked away.

I was praying that no one would come in off the road because you could still smell gun smoke in the air. Ronnie looked at me and asked, "What are we going to do about that big hole in the wall?"

I replied, "What is this we stuff? You shot the damn hole in the wall. Do you have a mouse in your pocket or what?"

He responded, "The sheriff will fire me for sure."

I laughed and said, "Now, Barney, you know Andy ain't going to fire you." Then reality set in—the big sheriff might fire my butt too.

My quick-thinking mind went into survival mode. Suddenly it hit me. We needed a quick fix to buy some time. I sent Ronnie to the kitchen to get some flour, while I went to the basement to get some of the leftover light green paint. We've got to work fast!

I remembered how the sweet little ole cook used to mix up her biscuit dough. We quickly got everything together, and I started mixing the dough, while Barney started mixing the paint. I quickly patched that three-inch bullet hole with my world-famous bullet hole patch, still praying that no one would come in. As soon as I gotter packed good, Ronnie slapped on the new green paint job. We both backed up and looked at the wall, me with biscuit dough all over my hands and him holding the can of paint and a brush, and stood there for a second and admired our quick fix. I let out a sigh of relief. "Boy, that looks great. Now let's hurry and get this cleaned up before someone comes in." My ole buddy left, still sweating blood as he headed home.

About thirty minutes later, the High Sheriff himself drove up in front of the office. I am thinking, *Oh my, that paint is still wet!* He walked in and said, "Hello, Jeff." Then he walked straight into the kitchen to get a cup of that good ole jailhouse coffee.

The sheriff walked up to the counter, leaned over, looked straight at me, and said, "You know, I can still smell that paint from when they painted this office a couple of weeks back."

I didn't even look up. I just grunted, "Yep."

Around five o'clock in the afternoon a few weeks later, I pulled into the sheriff's office. None of the other deputies were around. Ronnie was working the desk, and the office staff was gone. I got a cup of coffee and walked back to the front office. I set the coffee on the counter, and Ronnie said, "Turn around and take a look at the wall." I knew something had to be wrong by the sound of his voice. At first, I didn't see what he was talking about. I had almost forgotten about the biscuit hole. Oh no! That world-famous biscuit patch was drying out.

The three-inch hole was getting lighter in color. I turned around and looked at him, and he looked haggard and defeated. I said, "What are you going to do?"

Ronnie replied in a sad voice, "I just got to tell him."

I said, "Just make sure y'all are alone. Maybe he won't fire us."

The next day, around four thirty in the afternoon, I went to the office to gas up. I noticed four or five patrol cars were there, as well as the office staff. As I walked through the door, everyone started laughing and clapping their hands. The sheriff said, "Damn, Jeff, I wish I had you around when I shot that hole in the upstairs floor a few years ago with my new .45 automatic." We all had a big laugh. No one ever let Barney live it down!

Ronnie later transferred to the Sumter County Sheriff's Office and made a good detective. He was a good man and a good law enforcement officer. We were good friends until the end.

COUNTRY PREACHER CATCHES THE DEVIL

Sheriff Sim L. Lowman was contacted by the FBI advising we would be housing a federal prisoner on a charge of escaping the State Road Camp, south of Brooksville, while awaiting trial. The FBI also advised this federal prisoner was a real bad dude serving ninety-nine years to life in a federal prison in Atlanta, Georgia. This guy was very slick and had escaped several institutions.

After being in the Hernando County Jail for approximately a month on the escape charge, the federal prisoner, Don Tillis, made his move. The morning jailer was making his rounds and found Tillis missing from the head count. Chief jailer, Ron Elliott, contacted Sheriff Lowman. It was believed at the time; Tillis had used a comb and razor blades to fashion a hacksaw type tool. The rough tool was found on the floor near the window where he had climbed out of the County Jail. The escapee was five feet, eleven inches and 235 pounds with blond hair and blue eyes. A BOLO was immediately put out to all the surrounding counties.

About eight thirty in the morning, Ernie Chatman Sr. called Sheriff Lowman to advise him that his Buick Car Dealership on 41 South had been broken into during the night and that a new Buick was missing along with a .357 Smith & Wesson handgun.

This guy was a badass with nothing to lose. Serving ninety-nine years to life gave him plenty of time to think about how to escape and run. Now the "big manhunt" was on.

The sheriff called everyone out, even the posse that was headed up by Deputy Jeff Duval. Lots of other counties joined in the hunt, along with local male citizens who had guns and horses.

As nightfall came, the entire county was on edge. It was apparent that they weren't going to find him that day. As the darkness crept in, so did the fear of the citizens around the county. Every dog bark and every noise outside became Tillis in their minds, and the panic was on. Sightings were coming in from everywhere. It was impossible for the officers to keep up with the calls, even with the help of law enforcement officers from the surrounding counties and state officers. We had all the main roads blocked. The posse was brought in, and Jeff took Billy Donn and two other officers to patrol with him. The sound of the bloodhounds moving through the darkness was eerie.

Don Tillis's rap sheet was long, including aggravated assault on a law enforcement officer, attempted murder, armed robbery, and a few more crimes. We all were concerned that with his long rap sheet, he might kill someone to stay free.

During the first night, several sightings were called in, but nothing was found. All the officers were exhausted. Things began to slow down around four o'clock that morning. Jeff was sitting on a dirt road watching to see if anyone would cross it and hoping to catch a new track. About daylight, Deputy Richard Clay (75 was Richard's ID) called on the radio to the sheriff (70 was the sheriff's ID).

"75 to 70."

"Go ahead," replied the sheriff.

Clay asked, "What time are we going in?"

The sheriff responded, "When you bring Tillis's ass to jail. That is when you are going in." Then there was complete silence.

Later that morning, Sheriff Lowman called everyone to the dealership and set up a command post. Coffee and sandwiches were provided to all the law enforcement officers involved in the manhunt. At this time, the sheriff stood up on the back of a truck and advised everyone that Tillis had a car, was heavily armed, and would kill anyone who tried to stop him. Tillis was armed and dangerous.

As the second day dragged on, the men were showing signs of fatigue. They were going on twenty-four hours with no rest or decent food. According to the sheriff, they weren't going to get any rest.

*****

The posse was called back out, and my butt was still sore from riding that horse all day. One ole cracker cowboy, Milton Pollard, who was the foreman for Lykes Brother's cattle company in Brooksville, Florida, rode up next to me, looked over at me with a smirky smile, and asked me, "How does that saddle feel this morning, Mr. Deputy?" If I hadn't been friends with ole Pollard for so long, I would have slapped his hat right off his head, but I knew the golden rule, "Never mess with a cowboy's hat!"

The new Buick that had been stolen from the dealership was found abandoned and out of gas. Tillis was now on foot. For some reason, the bloodhounds could not follow Don Tillis's scent.

As darkness fell again, the men were extremely worn out. Red Brass, Buddy Brass, and Danny Spencer, Red's son-in-law, were out when they saw someone walking south of town. As they got closer, Red pulled alongside the guy to check him out. At which time, Don Tillis turned quickly and pointed a .357 Magnum in Red's face and said, "Y'all get out. I want the patrol car."

Red Brass asked, "Are you willing to kill us to get the car?"

Tillis replied, "Don't push me, or you'll find out!"

The three men let Don Tillis have the patrol car. Danny was locked in the back in the cage and kept yelling, "Let me out, Red!" The deputies managed to get to a phone and called in that Tillis now had a patrol car. The high sheriff was hot because he knew that Tillis wanted to kill him from prior scrapes they had in the past. Sheriff Lowman rolled south in a big 400 Buick Wildcat. It wasn't long before he spotted Tillis in the county patrol car. The chase was on! Lowman was catching up to Tillis with that Wildcat just screaming. Tillis was not the driver that the sheriff was. It wasn't long before Tillis lost control and rolled the county car over in the road. The sheriff was able to skid to a stop a safe distance back. Seeing that Tillis was out of the car, the sheriff started running toward the wreckage. Tillis had gotten his wish, a chance to kill Sheriff Lowman. Tillis fired the first shot, missing the sheriff. The sheriff returned fire but also missed. Tillis had managed to get into the woods. The sheriff jumped on his radio calling all units to assist and to bring the dogs. They were approximately four miles south of Brooksville.

The sheriff decided to run back out of the woods because he knew Tillis would ambush and kill him if given the opportunity. The adrenaline was running wild in all that were involved in the manhunt. The state dogs were put on a hot track, but they didn't know all of Tillis's tricks when he was on the run. Nor did Jeff until about five years later.

Tillis was moving north, back toward the Brooksville city limits, but he moved like a snake in the woods. The state dogs were no match for this convict. He was running them to death. The dogs were given a rest back at the State Road Camp truck. They then decided to put the Pasco County's best tracking dog on the trail, along with the best foot tracker I had ever seen, Brother Dave Stevens. Brother Stevens, also known as Preacher, was a local Baptist preacher, a part-time deputy, half Indian, and a cowboy.

It now had been three days, and they were entering the third night without sleep or rest, but the preacher seemed to be on a hot trail. Everyone was getting excited as we moved toward a junkyard just south of Brooksville. Jeff stayed behind the preacher and ole Howler, a big red bloodhound, as they made their way through the junkyard in the dark. Preacher and ole Howler were on the scent and knew that the devil was close by. The sheriff ordered the rest of the men to move in closer. Preacher called Jeff to assist him with the dog, as he got closer to the devil. They knew Tillis had tried to kill the sheriff earlier and was still armed. Jeff was following behind the duo holding his .41 Magnum down by his side. Preacher was holding a flashlight and the dog at the same time. When the preacher looked inside an old car, he came eye to eye with the devil himself. That bloodhound had missed ole Satan's scent. Preacher jumped back and yelled, "Jeff, I got him!" Jeff didn't know who was more scared, the preacher or the devil, but Jeff was glad that after three days and nights of hunting, the devil was caught.

Don Tillis was booked into the Hernando County Jail. Little did Jeff know then that their paths would cross again five years later. Brother Dave Stevens, the ole country preacher and part-time lawman, went back to preaching full time.

One night, while he was out riding patrol with Jeff, he told him he hoped the Lord would let him preach until the end. The ole country preacher nearly got his wish. He would preach holding himself up by the pulpit. The Lord called him home one evening with his family by his side.

Jeff had lost one of the best friends that he ever had, and the memories of them wrangling, hunting, and rounding up cattle in the Annutteliga Hammock, northwest of Brooksville, came rushing back. Jeff will never forget those days and spending time with the ole country preacher, Red Brass, Danny Spencer, and Doug Chorvat Sr. Just a bunch of good ole cracker cowboys and lawmen who loved the Hammock.

NINETY-NINE YEARS TO LIFE WITH NOTHING TO LOSE

A new sheriff came to town. Chief Deputy Melvin R. Kelly defeated Sheriff Sim L. Lowman, his longtime boss, by a large majority.

The influx of the Yankees from the North had changed politics quickly in Hernando County.

One morning, Sheriff Kelly called Deputy Jeff Duval into his office and asked him with a smile, "How do you like that new police package '73 Dodge Coronet?"

Jeff replied, "It's the best patrol car I've had so far. I love it!"

At which time, the sheriff said, "Well, you're going to get to take it for a long ride."

Jeff was puzzled and asked, "How's that, Sheriff?"

Sheriff Kelly then responded by saying, "I've chosen you to go to Marion Illinois State Penitentiary to get Don L. Tillis. I have a bench warrant that you will take with you, but first we're going to outfit that new Dodge with a special built cage just for Tillis. Take the car down to Troy's Welding Shop. The cage is ready to be put into the car. Also, I have a special deputy assigned to go along on the trip to ride shotgun."

Three days later, the two officers met at the county sheriff's office at six o'clock in the morning. They received their instructions from the sheriff and given the bench warrant issued by one of the circuit judges in the Fifth Judicial Circuit for the extradition of Tillis and to bring his body before the court in Hernando County. The sheriff advised they would pick up Tillis at the sheriff's office in Marion,

Illinois, on Friday morning at eight o'clock. The sheriff further stated to be very careful with the subject. "You know his record. They are housing him in the east wing of the Marion State Penitentiary. That's where they keep the meanest and the baddest of the baddest." The two officers left the sheriff's office heading north about seven o'clock in the morning to begin their long drive to Marion, Illinois. The two deputies were aware of Tillis's rap sheet and record. He was a hardened criminal and escape artist. Jeff knew him very well after hunting him for three days and nights without a break. He would be careful and keep one eye on this mean bad guy.

The first day was long, about nine hours. About four thirty in the afternoon, the two officers arrived in Nashville during the worse ice and snowstorm that Tennessee had seen in twenty years. Neither one of these ole Florida boys had ever driven in snow or ice before but did have fun the next morning at the Holiday Inn, throwing snowballs at each other around the patrol car before hitting the road heading for Marion. Jeff was very cautious as big chunks of ice were falling from trees and power lines, and the edges of the road were iced over, but the Dodge handled it well since it had fat tires and limited slip rear end.

Sometime around dark, they arrived and checked into a motel in Marion, Illinois. Jeff contacted the sheriff's office in Marion that evening and advised they would pick up Tillis at the county jail about eight o'clock the next morning.

When Jeff and Sonny arrived at the sheriff's office in Marion, they waited approximately half an hour and was placed in a 12 × 12 cell for Don L. Tillis to be brought in by two state guards.

Jeff heard the rattling of chains coming down the hallway. When the door opened, the two guards escorted Tillis into the cell block. He had a hood over his head, belly chain, and handcuffs with chains running down to his leg shackles. It was then Jeff realized the seriousness and responsibility he had been given by the sheriff to bring the bad man back to Florida.

One of the state guards spoke up and said, "We will take our chains off but leave the hood on. Do you want us to place your chains on him?"

Jeff replied, "No, I want to do it myself as soon as I read the bench warrant to him. Take the hood off his head a minute." Jeff looked Tillis straight in the eye and read the warrant, which said, "Bring Don L. Tillis's body before the Court. Jeff said, "Don, do you understand what this means? It means I'm going to take you back to Florida with this warrant. It says your body. It's up to you how you arrive, but your body will be taken back to Florida by me, one way or another. Do you understand?"

He replied, "Yes, I do."

Jeff said, "Don, I chased your ass for three days and nights without sleep. Do you understand it doesn't make any difference to me how you get there, dead or alive? It's up to you." Jeff then put the chains, handcuffs, and leg irons on Tillis. Jeff and Sonny and the other two guards walked Tillis to the patrol car. Once he was seated in the back of the Dodge, Jeff took the hood off his head. Tillis looked around the cage. It was wrapped to the top of the car and all the way around the inside of the car. There was no way to penetrate through the cage.

Tillis also noticed and said, "Jeff, your pretty heavily armed," when he saw Jeff's M1 carbine with a fifty-round clip in the bottom gun rack and a short twelve-gauge double-barrel shotgun in the top rack in front of the cage. Jeff had learned quickly to use a little psychology when necessary.

As the three headed south out of Marion, Tillis was quiet. About three or four hours later, he began to talk a little bit about his criminal history. Things were settling in on the long trip back to Florida.

About four and half hours into the drive, Jeff decided to stop at a fast-food restaurant. He asked Don if he wanted to get out to eat. The prisoner replied, "No, I'm not getting out." Sonny went into the restaurant, and Jeff stood outside and talked to Tillis. Just a casual conversation. Jeff knew that the fox was trying to cozy up to the hound. They sat under the shade of a tree and ate, and it wasn't long before they were back on the road. Sonny drove until they reached Tennessee, and then Jeff took over at the state line arriving in Nashville about six thirty in the evening.

The weather was very cold as Jeff pulled into the Nashville Metro Jail so they could house the prisoner overnight. As they pulled into the sally port, Tillis looked back to see the doors closing behind him. A guard met them in the sally port, and Don L. Tillis was escorted to a single cell. Once out of Tillis's sight, Jeff explained to the guard to have an all-night guard watch Tillis until he was to be picked up at eight o'clock in the morning or Tillis wouldn't be there the next morning.

The guard said, "Who is this guy, Houdini?"

Jeff replied, "You're exactly right. He is an escape artist with several escapes under his belt, and he is a very dangerous man serving ninety-nine years to life with nothing to lose."

The two deputies drove to the Holiday Inn in Nashville to get a room for the night. As they started inside, they could see the swimming pool was frozen over. Jeff said, "Sonny, I don't know about you, but this cracker is cold." Sonny just laughed as they walked into the Holiday Inn. The two deputies settled in and got a good night's sleep.

The next morning, they arrived at the metro jail about seven thirty to pick up the prisoner. He had been served breakfast and was ready to be chained up. Jeff put the chains and shackles on Don, just like he had the day before. Jeff was thinking in his mind, *This fox doesn't know his way around a wiry hound.* After checking the chains and shackles twice, they loaded Tillis and headed south.

About three thirty in the afternoon, Jeff pulled into a drive-in restaurant. "Don, are you hungry?"

Don answered, "I sure am, Jeff."

"I'm going to escort you into the restaurant and let you eat inside."

Don replied, "There is no way in hell I'm getting out of this car."

"Suit yourself."

Once again Sonny went into the restaurant and ordered three box lunches to go and headed south once more. Jeff let the other two men eat while he continued to drive. Later, they switched drivers so Jeff could eat his meal on the go.

He decided to drive straight through, taking his time and keeping an eye on this dangerous prisoner sitting two feet behind him. They had the light taped so only the back seat would be lit and they could watch this dangerous outlaw as darkness fell. Jeff advised Sonny to turn sideways in the seat so he could keep an eye on Tillis the rest of the night.

They drove along at a slower pace in the darkness. He could feel the danger and was a little on the edge wondering what this criminal was plotting. He knew that Tillis was thinking how he could get out and run, if given the opportunity. He believed Tillis was thinking about the armor in front of that cage and was probably thinking about what Jeff had said about taking his body before the court.

Approximately an hour later that night, they pulled into a roadside car hop for coffee. The young lady served them coffee on a tray. Jeff and Sonny stood outside the car to stretch their legs.

Once outside the car door, Jeff said, "Don, do you want to stand up and stretch your legs?"

He said, "No way!"

It was then Jeff began to think his plan was working on this dangerous felon. After standing up for about ten minutes out in the cold night air, they switched drivers as Sonny took the wheel heading south once more. About daybreak, they stopped after crossing the Florida State Line for coffee to go.

Tillis had started opening up a lot, telling the two officers how he had outsmarted everyone all these years. He told them how he would run a dog in the ground by putting black pepper in his socks that he would get from a trustee. He said a dog wouldn't follow that scent, and sometimes he would backtrack ten to fifteen yards in the same tracks and then take another direction in case the dogs caught a slight scent. Don said he would also climb a tree that was close to another tree and then jump to the next tree and grab a limb and swing out, leaving a large area with no tracks.

As they began to get close to Raiford, they came to a fork in the road. Jeff played a little mind game with the prisoner. Jeff said, "Sonny, do we go left or right here? I'm not sure."

Tillis spoke up and said, "Jeff, you go left if you're going to Raiford. I know where I'm at."

The sly old hound knew better, and he thought, *Well, that was Don's last thought of escape, if he could get me away from Raiford.*

Don said, "Do you remember me cutting my way out of the jail with a hacksaw I made with a comb and razor blades?"

Jeff replied, "Yes! Everybody wondered how you did that. It was in the newspaper how you fashioned a comb and razor blades into a hacksaw."

Tillis laughed. "Are those people still eating that turkey?" And he laughed.

Jeff said, "Some people are. I never believed it. How did you really saw out?"

He replied, "I guess I can tell you now after all these years. I talked a trustee into getting me a hacksaw blade. Once I got a bar cut, I would fill it up with soap and leave it in place. The next night, I would move out to the next cell door and do the same thing until I was ready to go. The night I escaped, I simply removed three bars from each door until it was out. I had lost enough weight that I could squeeze through. Once I got to the storeroom, I crawled out the window and was on my way."

About five miles north of the Florida State Prison in Raiford, Florida, Don Tillis asked Jeff, "How is my ole sheriff friend, Sim L. Lowman?"

Jeff chuckled. "Don, Sheriff Lowman retired a few years ago."

He said, "Who is the sheriff?"

Jeff replied, "Melvin Kelly is the sheriff."

Don exclaimed, "Melvin Kelly!"

Jeff asked, "Yeah, why?"

They drove through the gate at Raiford, and once the gate was closing, Tillis said, "I'll be damned! That's why you left these chains and shackles on where you knew I could get out of them and try to run."

Jeff said, "That's right. You see, Don, you're not the only fox in the woods. A little psychology goes a long way."

Don said, "Yeah, that's true, but I damn sure thought Sim L. sent you after me, and you were going to let me make an escape attempt and kill me on the way back to Raiford."

Jeff said, "Why's that?"

"With you reading the warrant like you did, leaving the chains on, making it easy for me to get out of them and making sure you had a lot of firepower, I truly believed that Sheriff Lowman had sent you up on a mission to take me out. I was convinced Sheriff Sim Lowman had instructed you to let me escape and kill me in the attempt because I tried to kill Lowman in the past. I got to give you credit, Jeff."

Jeff replied, "No hard feelings, I hope. I'm just doing my job. I hope someday you get your life straight. I wish you the best of luck."

As Tillis stepped out in the sally port at the Florida State Prison, the lawman and the outlaw shook hands and went their separate ways. Forty-seven years later when this story was written, retired lieutenant Jeff Duval wonders if Don Lee Tillis is still serving ninety-nine years to life or if his life has ended in prison.

GHOST BOOGERS AND OTHER STRANGE THINGS

Most people have no idea what a deputy sheriff sees in a long career. Here are just a few things that I am going to share with you.

West of town are three historic cemeteries located in a heavily wooded hammock area, full of mossy oaks and palmettos, all three within walking distance of one another. One old black cemetery was on the east side of the road, a Confederate cemetery on the west side of the road, and a private family cemetery on the north side of the road—all dating back to the early 1800s and some even earlier than that in the private family cemetery. Some people had said that ghosts had been seen in the area and strange sounds at night had been heard.

One stormy, windy night, lightning was flashing, and my ole buddy Billy Donn was dispatched out to the black cemetery. Now, Billy Donn had no fear. Some said he didn't have enough sense to fear anything. It was raining, and the wind was swaying the moss in the oak trees when he arrived in the deep woods. Billy Donn called Brooksville and asked for a backup, which was unusual for him. It seemed that Billy had seen something that made even him uneasy. He called me and said, "Sarge, can you come out here?"

When I arrived in the deep woods, I saw Billy Donn's car sitting just inside the gates of the old cemetery. He had his bright lights on and was still sitting in his car. I pulled up behind Billy Donn's patrol car. He was still sitting there. I got out of his car and got into Billy Donn's car to get out of the rain and wind.

Billy looked over at me wide-eyed with the inside lights on. I could see that he was uneasy. Billy Donn said, "Look up the hill, Sarge. What is that sitting there?"

As I strained to see through the cemetery, I replied, "Man, that looks like a coffin, Billy. Go up there and check it out." I was just kind of messin' with Mr. Tough Guy.

Billy Donn said, "Come on!"

I replied, "I'm pulling rank tonight. It's raining. You go and let me know what it is."

Now ole Billy Donn was a big boy and walked with a John Wayne swagger, but not tonight. He started walking up the sand road in the graveyard. The moss was swaying, the wind was howling, and lightning was flashing. Billy was holding his flashlight in one hand, and his other hand was on his gun butt. Billy Donn was about halfway up the road, so I eased the outside speaker on and gave out a ghostly moan. Big bad Billy Donn jumped straight up, and it looked like about four feet high, spinning and screaming like a little girl.

I spoke into the outside speaker again, "Billy, did you see a booger?"

Billy Donn ran halfway back to the car and then suddenly realized what had happened. He then called me a few choice bad names and said, "Sarge, get your butt out here too."

With that, I got out of the car laughing and walked up to him and said, "Do you want the sarge to hold your hand, boy?"

Billy Donn replied, "You smart-ass!"

As we walked closer, we could see that the box was open. I'll admit what we saw made me uneasy too—a large male body was inside with his hands pulled straight up.

Billy Donn said, "What kind of crazy person would do something like this?"

I replied, "Billy, you are gonna find out in years to come that only we live in the real world. You are going to see a lot of things on this job that you never dreamed of."

We called dispatch and asked them to call the local funeral home to pick up the corpse and transport to the funeral home in town. I advised Billy Donn to contact the family of the deceased.

Later we had a laugh together about me funnin' him at such a time. I said, "Son, it's a way of coping with the job. If you don't mix it up, you'll go crazy."

*****

The old Confederate cemetery was located across the road. All the headstones were marked with the name, rank, and unit that the Confederate soldiers had served in. This cemetery was thick with palmettos that had grown up over the years.

Now, as all Southerners know, rattlesnakes love palmetto patches. Jeff broke off a large stick to make his way through the palmettos into the cemetery. He had played in this cemetery many times as a young boy years ago. As Jeff looked through the graveyard, he saw an open grave and knew that they would have to fill it back in. He then called dispatch and asked for two inmates to be brought out with shovels. When they arrived, he noticed the walking boss and two young inmates. As they got out of the truck with the walking boss, they were laughing and in a playful mood. As they came through the palmettos, Jeff said, "Watch out for the rattlesnakes. They love palmettos!"

The walking boss knew Jeff well and knew that he was up to something. The boys kept laughing and joking around as they came closer. One of the boys said, "We ain't scared of no snakes or any Confederate ghosts."

When they got about ten feet from the open grave, Jeff yanked up a big five-foot diamondback rattlesnake from out of the palmettos that he had caught before they had arrived. The two young inmates yelled and ran like rabbits through a thicket.

The ole walking boss said, "Damn, Jeff, now they won't come back," as Jeff spat chewing tobacco on top of the rattlesnake's head as it crawled off.

About a half hour later, one of the fellas yelled, "Where is that snake?"

Jeff replied, "Aww, hell, y'all come on back. You ain't scared of no snakes or Confederate ghosts remember."

He also remembered one strange full moon night he was patrolling on Centralia Road going east. It was as straight as a Seminole arrow through the hammock. It was well graded and wide. The deputies sometimes used the road to practice maneuvers, reverse spins, and others. Sometimes when the moon was full, he would ease along with his headlights off. It was something he had learned early in his career. You can slip up on a bad guy with your lights off. Sometimes Jeff caught them in the midst of committing a crime. These things usually happened after midnight, about two or three o'clock in the morning. He would ease toward his house off Highway 491 to do a walk-around and check on his family. Moving slowly along, he would roll the window down to smell the fresh cool hammock air.

One night, he noticed something sparkle way up the road in the moonlight. Moving slowly eastward, he knew something was in the road. Not knowing what was up ahead, he called dispatch and asked for a backup. There was only one other deputy on besides him, and there was no telling where he was.

Jeff picked up the mike and said, "11 to 60."

The deputy replied, "Go ahead, 11."

Jeff asked, "What is your location, Billy?" He advised that he was in the Spring Lake Area. "How about heading my way. We got something out here on Centralia Road." He knew that Billy was at least thirty miles away, but he eased up on the vehicle and couldn't believe his eyes. "11 to Brooksville."

"Go ahead, 11."

"Gene, you will never believe what I come up on out here."

Gene said, "Knowing you, it won't surprise me. What is it?"

"A new hearse with a crowd of people standing around in the road." Jeff said, "Step it up, Billy. Bring it on," as Jeff sat watching them with his binoculars. They didn't know that he was watching them.

As the crowd saw the patrol car easing up in the moonlight, they began moving out of the road. Jeff let the window down about a quarter of the way. His .357 Smith & Wesson was under his right leg already. He was thinking, *I am not going to have one of these freaks grab me through the window! What kind of nuts are standing around a hearse on a dirt road at three o'clock in the morning?* Jeff stopped behind and just to the left of the hearse about thirty feet. One cockeyed fellow walked over. Jeff had his Smith & Wesson ready to go with his right hand on it. After all, this might be a hearse load of vampires and freaks. This just ain't normal! He didn't know what to watch closer, mister cockeyed freak or the rest of those zombies walking around his patrol car.

"Step it up, Billy!"

Brooksville called a radio check, "Are you 10-4?"

His reply was, "So far."

At this point in time, he ran a stolen check and registration on the hearse. It was registered to a funeral home in Tampa. Then he looked at the cockeyed dude standing outside the window. He asked him if there was a body in the hearse, like he was going to tell him the truth, if there was.

He said, "No, there is no body in the hearse."

Jeff thought to himself, *What kind of club is this, freaks, nuts, and weirdos?* He was thinking that Billy was only a couple of miles away now.

The cockeyed freak said to Jeff's amazement, "We are here near these large power lines waiting for the UFOs to fuel up."

Jeff said, "Aww, heck, brother, you missed it. They were here last night!" Now he knew that the badge and the oath were saying, "You have to get out of the car and see what's in that hears."

As Billy was pulling up, he was thinking, *If one of them freak vampires get you, ole Billy will get here, or maybe we can scare them away before daylight.*

When Jeff checked the hearse out, it was empty. He said, "Billy, just keep thinking about what I told you in the past. Only a law enforcement officers live in the real world. The common man has no clue what we see."

Billy was checking out some of those pretty little vampires, as he would. Jeff eased over to Billy and said, "Be careful there, buddy. One of those young cuties may want to nibble on your neck, and that would be deadly." The cockeyed freak's story checked out, and with this, Jeff said, "Billy, let's get the heck away from here!"

As Jeff drove into his driveway on Highway 491, it was breaking daylight, and he felt safe, because vampires don't like the daylight, right?

THE MEN TIME FORGOT

One evening while sitting around the campfire with Gov. Lawton Chiles and another ole Florida cracker, Sheriff Jamie Adams of Sumter County, Jeff recalled the story of Bill Brayton, deputy sheriff of Hernando County, that was shot.

Jeff said he was working twelve-hour shifts from six o'clock in the evening till six o'clock in the morning. He said he would work the central part of the county as far east as the Sumter County Line on Highway 50 and everything north and south. Bill Brayton was the only other deputy working with Jeff on the midnight shift. Brayton usually worked the west side of the county.

Jeff received a call on old Crystal River Road for an attempted arson at a local contractor's home about nine o'clock one Friday night. When he arrived at the residence of the complainant, he was met by the victim, Jim Hagert, outside the house. When Jeff stepped out of his patrol car, Jim told him he believed his business partner, Ted Wilson, had tried to set his house on fire and was seen running from the yard with a five-gallon can back toward his home about sixty yards away, because the two lived next door to each other.

It was because the business was going belly up and the two had been feuding over how to settle the business. Ted Wilson was unhappy with the settlement the court had set down and swore vengeance on Jim Hagert.

Jeff drove over to Ted Wilson's home. It was totally dark, and no one answered the door. After he searched around the victim's home, no signs of foul play were found. Since he did not see any signs of foul play himself and all he had was Jim Hagert's story, no other action would be taken that night. Jeff told Jim Hagert that he was going to hang out in the area for a while in the dark that night. Nothing else occurred that night. He continued his usual duties later that night, ending his shift at six o'clock in the morning. He was scheduled to be off the next night, which was Saturday.

He was called out about eleven o'clock Saturday night by the Hernando County Sheriff's Office Dispatch to aid in the shooting of Deputy Bill Brayton. When Jeff and Deputy Moore arrived on the scene, the ambulance was leaving with Deputy Brayton. Jim Hagert's house was ablaze. The city police and Florida Highway Patrol arrived to assist with the shooting. "Officer Brayton was down." There was a shoot-out between Brayton and Ted Wilson when Brayton confronted him with a can of fuel.

When Brayton arrived, he saw Wilson setting fire to the house with a torch and fuel. Ted Wilson ran from the scene, out to Old Crystal River Road. Brayton had county K-9 Smokey and had turned the dog loose to catch Ted Wilson as he fled the scene toward his car out front.

Brayton was always a crack shot on the range and carried a seven-inch .357 Smith & Wesson Magnum, and he called it Gertrude. Jeff said he remembered a conversation between him and Brayton over coffee in reference to a firing range and an actual shoot-out. Jeff said he remembered telling Bill it's a lot different when someone was shooting at you than it was shooting at a target. At that point in time, neither Bill nor Jeff ever thought they would live to see this narrative come into play and that it would ever play out in the years to come!

That night, when Wilson ran from the house, there was a small station wagon, approximately forty yards in an open field. Wilson got to the car before Smokey, the K-9, caught him. Wilson stood behind the door of the Dodson and took his first shot at Deputy Bill Brayton, striking him above the left ear, with the bullet lodged in the skull at the base of his neck, knocking him to the ground.

Bill Brayton was able to return fire with big "Gert" but never hit Wilson. The dog returned to Brayton, lying on the ground bleeding. Brayton was able to get to his car to call for help. Ted Wilson fled the scene unscathed. Jeff asked dispatch to put out a Bolo immediately, "Be on the lookout, statewide, for a Dodson station wagon, Ted

Wilson was driving." The fire department was summoned. Everyone, including the sheriff, was called out, but the suspect was not to be found. The home was lost!

Jeff escaped being injured again or a possible tragedy for himself only because he had Saturday night off. He really wanted to catch Wilson because he and Bill Brayton were friends for many years and had worked as a team.

Bill Brayton stayed a few days in Lykes Memorial Hospital, where he was treated for a bullet in the head. The doctors said it was too dangerous to remove the bullet from his head, and he was sent home to rest for a few days.

The average person has no idea what it's like to be in a gun battle unless you've been there.

Jeff drove to Bill's house one afternoon to visit his longtime friend and to see how he was recuperating. When Jeff knocked on the door, he heard Bill say, "Who is it?"

"It's me Bill, Jeff."

He said, "Just a minute."

When Bill came to the door, he had the big gun in his hand. This was something only a law enforcement officer will understand. Once you have been shot at or shot, this was something you will never forget. That's why Brayton came to the door with a gun. It's called post-traumatic stress disorder (PTSD).

Brayton lay back down on the couch and laid Gert on the coffee table next to him. Jeff sat down in a chair next to the couch. The two men began to talk about all the years they had known each other. Brayton was a city officer when Jeff was in his midteens. He always liked Bill. He remembered when Bill and his brothers all played for the Hernando High School Fighting Leopards.

Bill Brayton had stopped Jeff and his friends one night for speeding through town on their motorcycles, heading to Louie's Bowling Alley to see their girlfriends. Brayton had stopped them because Jeff didn't have a headlight, but Bill cut him slack by letting him park his motorcycle at the sheriff's office on Jefferson Street. Jeff rode with Billy Cook and the rest of their buddies to the bowling alley. Jeff never forgot the break Bill gave him that night and liked him from then on.

*****

It's funny what you think about when you see your friend lying on the couch with a bullet hole in his head. That could have been me. If I had not had the night off that night, I would have been sent to that same location again for the second time. Who knows if I would have gone home because I would have been dispatched?

*****

The two visited for about an hour. Bill retold the story. Jeff listened trying to visualize what happened that night and why the K-9 never caught Ted Wilson before he got to the car. Bill had no answer. As Jeff got ready to leave his friend, he assured him he would be there for him, and no matter what, he would stand by his side.

In 1972, Hernando County only had seven road deputies. They were a close-knit group, like a family, and worked long hard hours with very little pay. At this point, Bill had about sixteen years' experience in law enforcement.

As Jeff stood up to leave, he turned around and looked at Bill with that big gun Gertrude, lying on the coffee table and said, "I love you, brotherman. When do you think you will be coming back to work?"

Bill Brayton looked at him straight in the eye without any emotion and replied, "I won't be coming back. I'm done."

Jeff said, "Bill, I completely understand. You've been a damn good officer for a very long time."

As Jeff drove away, he knew he would miss his friend, Deputy William H. Brayton, a good officer who was shot in the line of duty and lived to tell the story.

VINNIE HAD CONNECTIONS

Now, Vinnie Scanio sounds Italian, and that he was. He came up to Brooksville about 1976 and opened a grocery store west of Brooksville. Most of his items in the store were scratch and dent that he would pick up in Tampa once a week.

Vinnie came into the sheriff's office one day on a complaint and wanted to speak directly to the sheriff. He was escorted into the sheriff's office, and they talked about an hour and must have hit it off right away. They were close friends for many years after that. Jeff, one of the longtime local deputies, became good friends with Vinnie as well. It seemed like every time Vinnie needed something, he would call on Jeff and would often ride with Jeff during a weekend or sometimes at night.

Jeff could tell that this Tampa Italian, at some point in his past, had known some big people in the "family." As they got to know each other better, he would call and ask for Duval to come by. By this time, Jeff had taken a liking for Vinnie. One night while riding with Jeff, Vinnie dropped some big-time names from the "family" in Hillsborough County. Jeff knew he was not "bullshitting" him. Jeff was pretty shrewd and could read people very well. He knew Vinnie walked the walk and talked the talk. He knew the names that Vinnie had dropped in their conversations were some big-time crime bosses. Scanio had told him he had connections all over Florida and up the East Coast, but he also knew Vinnie had been out of the "family" a long time.

One evening while they were out on patrol, Jeff told Vinnie he had received some threats against his family by a drug dealer. Vinnie looked over at the deputy and said in that Italian lingo, "Jeff, do you need some help with this problem? If you do, I can handle this for you because you're my friend."

Jeff thought, *Damn.* He knew what he meant but said, "No, not right now. I will let you know later, Vinnie." He knew he could not afford to get tangled up in something like this being a law enforcement officer. One had to handle these things quietly on their own. Jeff had been known to hold some prayer meetings with some local bigmouth who liked to talk. He also knew if anybody wanted to kill him, they wouldn't be talking about it, usually.

Scanio said, "Okay, but if you ever need help, Jeff, you've got it. You're my friend." Jeff knew what he meant but did not say anything the rest of the night.

One Sunday morning, Vinnie called the sheriff's office and asked for Jeff to come to his store located adjacent to a 7-Eleven. Vinnie parked his car at the back of his store after being out to the wee hours of the morning with some of his friends from Ybor City.

When Jeff arrived on the scene behind Vinnie's store, he noticed ole Vinnie walking back and forth between the two-story building looking at the ground. As Jeff stepped out of his patrol car, he yelled, "Hey, Scanio! What have you lost?" He could tell Vinnie looked very upset and haggard.

Vinnie replied, "I came in before daylight this morning, and I walked over to get some coffee at the 7-Eleven store. I think I must have lost my damn teeth!"

Jeff knew not to laugh, but it was hard to hold it back. "You lost your teeth!"

Vinnie said, "Yes, that's the last time I remember having them. They have to be between my door and the 7-Eleven store."

Jeff began a search for the missing teeth. He figured his ole friend had too much to drink with his buddies in Tampa and probably spit them out while walking over to the 7-Eleven, but no teeth were to be found after about an hour's search. Jeff said, "Vinnie, call me later if you find them."

About two o'clock that afternoon, Vinnie called the sheriff's office and asked for Jeff to give him a call. Once arriving back at the sheriff's office, Jeff called Vinnie back. Jeff asked, "What's up, Vinnie?"

Vinnie said, "Well, I found my damn teeth."

"Where were they?"

"I kept looking around the backyard and evidentially my dog Rocky found them when you and I couldn't and the SOB found them and dug a hole and buried them. I saw where he had been digging, and I checked the hole and found them. Can you believe the damn dog had my teeth?"

When Jeff told Sheriff Kelly about Vinnie's lost teeth, they both laughed so hard they cried and never let Vinnie Scanio live the story down. Jeff told Vinnie, "I bet that dog looked good wearing your teeth."

This was nothing compared to another weekend when he went down to see his buddies in Ybor. He came home from Ybor after having dinner with his "family" and enjoying some of the fine Cuban cigars made in Ybor City. He would always bring Jeff one or two and give them to him when he would do a ride along. Jeff knew the old man was lonely, and that was why he took up time with Vinnie and he enjoyed his stories of the old days in Tampa.

Vinnie was one of a kind. He never called Jeff by his first name. It was always Duval this or Duval that. Jeff didn't mind. When he would call the office, he would say, "Send Duval out here." Jeff always looked forward to seeing Vinnie and hearing what adventures he had in Hillsborough County that weekend.

Before I forget it, not only did he lose his teeth, but he also had called early one Sunday morning and said, "Send Duval out here. Someone stole my car." When Jeff arrived on the scene, Vinnie was pacing on the side of the property. Now, Vinnie was known to get a load on with his brothers before he would come back to Brooksville. This particular Sunday morning, Jeff pulled into Vinnie's side driveway of the scratch-and-dent store. Ole Vinnie was hot. He said, "Some SOB stole my car."

Jeff replied, "When was the last time you saw it?"

"I came home last night in it, and it was gone when I got up this morning."

"Okay, I'll look around for it. Go back inside and take it easy. I'll call you after a while." At which time, Vinnie went inside and said he would take a nap.

Knowing Vinnie like he did, Jeff decided to look around the area. Now, the 7-Eleven store was located about forty yards west of Vinnie's scratch-and-dent store.

Jeff decided before he started a lot of paperwork to look around the local area. Once Vinnie went inside to take a nap, Jeff started back to his patrol car and just decided to walk around back and look. Lo and behold, he looked over at the 7-Eleve, store, which was about forty yards from Vinnie's store. He could see a trail the old man used to walk back and forth. As he looked over, there sat Vinnie's big gray and black Oldsmobile sitting in front of the store. Jeff went on over to the store and asked the clerk how long the car had been sitting there. She said, "Vinnie came in right after I opened up this morning and got a cup of coffee and walked back over to the store. I knew he had been drinking. I decided to let the car stay. I knew he would find it later today." Jeff walked out and got in the Oldsmobile and drove over to Vinnie's and parked the car, leaving the keys in the ignition. He got into his patrol car and went on about his job that day.

About two o'clock that afternoon, Scanio called the sheriff's office and said, "Have Duval call me." When Jeff called, Vinnie answered the phone and said, "Duval, you're not going to believe this. The SOB brought my damn car back. He didn't go far because it still had gas in it."

He replied, "Well, Vinnie, he probably knew you were a dang gangster and that you would have him knocked off if he didn't bring the car back!"

Scanio laughed and said, "That's right!"

They both laughed. Jeff never told him any different. He didn't want to hurt the old man's feelings.

He thought a lot of old Vinnie. They rode many a night and both shared stories of their careers. Some of Vinnie's he would take to the grave. That's just the way it was.

Sheriff Kelly called Jeff into his office one day and asked him to sit down. He said, "Jeff, our old friend Vinnie passed away last night at home peacefully in his bed." Jeff never said a word. He just shook his head and walked out to his patrol car, thinking about his old friend Vinnie. He knew he would never forget the antics of old Vinnie and the fun times they had shared over the past few years. He can still see old Vinnie, digging up those teeth that his dog had buried years ago. He was a true friend to Jeff, and he knew I would have his back in a minute.

God bless Vinnie Scanio. May he rest in peace.

CHRISTER WOOD

Sgt. Jeff Duval shared a story about a young man that had a dream of becoming a Major League Baseball player.

Jeff said he was working the east side of the county in the spring of 1977 and remembered heading to the Ridge Manor Substation on the east side of the county that morning on Highway 50, east of I-75. He just happened to notice a silver car sitting on the riverbank below and alongside the river bridge of the Withlacoochee River. He said he didn't give it much thought and proceeded to the substation at Highway 301 and Highway 50.

As he walked into his office, he spoke to the dispatcher and said, "Good morning, Matt. Anything going on this morning?"

The dispatcher replied, "It's been pretty quiet, Sergeant."

With this, he proceeded to his office to check over the night radio log and deputy reports from the night before. It was an average morning. When he finished his paperwork, he decided to go back to the interstate and check the businesses and then proceed to the Eight Days Inn to have coffee and breakfast.

As Jeff was sitting at the table, he was thinking about the silver car he saw earlier that morning. It was still sitting below and along the side of the bridge near the Withlacoochee River. He just figured it was somebody fishing, as a lot of people would stop there to fish, which was not unusual. After having breakfast, he went about his normal patrol duties on the east side of the county. He decided to take a ride up I-75 to the Sumter County Line, where he met his old friend, Sgt. Travis Farmer, at the rest stop on the northbound lane so they could discuss some burglary cases that had crossed the county line. They would often get together with the other agencies to discuss some cases that their officers were working on.

After the meeting with Sergeant Farmer, Jeff decided to check out some information on a couple of bad guys that Sergeant Farmer had given him. The location of the home where the bad guys were located was south on Highway 301, heading toward what they called the French Quarter, which was Lachoochee. It was commonly known there were some people that lived in that area in the French Quarter that had sticky fingers back in those days.

Jeff said when he came off I-75, he headed west on Highway 50 toward Spring Lake to talk to a confidential informant that lived in the Spring Lake area, and then he headed home to take a short lunch break, where he lived in a wooded area off Mondon Hill Road about a mile north of Highway 50.

At approximately 12:30 p.m., Jeff took a 10-8, which meant he was back in service from lunch and on the road. As he crossed over the Withlacoochee River, he didn't notice the silver car but decided to check the area along the river off Cypress Drive that curved around like a snake along the river where there were a few weekend cabins and homes that needed to be checked. Occasionally, he would find a home or cabin that had been burglarized and would have his office contact the owner to come up and meet him at that location.

However, this day turned out to be an average day with no major problems other than a few minor calls.

He went home around six o'clock in the evening. If he was caught up in a call, he couldn't get off on time. When he got home, he enjoyed working with his horse, a young filly, that Mr. Dan Merritt had sold him. She was about four months old. He enjoyed working with the horse with halter training, exercising, and just in general spending time with the young filly. Also, he enjoyed working in his spring garden with his two young sons, Jeff and Avery. The boys really loved living in the country. They enjoyed working in the garden and being around their dad working the horse and playing with Spikie, a young English bulldog. The kids, the dog, and the horse would have a great day romping around the fields.

The next morning, he checked in on the radio about eight o'clock and advised Brooksville Dispatch that he was 10-8, which meant that he was in service on duty and headed to Brooksville's main office to gas up the patrol car and checked in with the sheriff and captain for a briefing and would usually have a couple of cups of jailhouse coffee with the guys and check with the dispatchers to see if they had any information for him.

Jeff said he would usually meet a trustee at the gas pump and chat with him for a few minutes because he knew most of the guys that were in jail as he was a local for so long. He remembered one morning a young trustee that he had befriended. Let's call him Drake. Drake was a funny young black man, always jolly, smiling, laughing, and cutting up. This morning, he asked Jeff if he could borrow $20. Jeff said he kind of looked at him sideways and smiled and said, "Drake, what you need $20 for in jail?"

Drake just smiled and laughed and said, "I really need it."

Jeff looked in his pocket and said, "Damn, Drake, this is the last $20 I got," but pulled it out and handed it to him.

Drake stuck it in his pocket and said, "Thank you," and kind of shuffled backward and laughed. At which time, Drake handed Jeff the $20 back. Jeff asked, "What's this about?" with a halfway smile.

Drake said, "I just wanted to see if you were really my friend."

The two men remained friends until Drake died about thirty-five years later. Jeff was really saddened when he heard the news that his old buddy was gone but had a lot of good memories of the times spent around the old county sheriff's office.

After leaving the gas pump and saying goodbye to Drake that morning, he headed east on Highway 50 to his office at the substation in Ridge Manor. Upon crossing the Withlacoochee River bridge, he got a glance of the silver car again but was in a hurry to get to the office. Once getting his paperwork done, he started his routine patrol of the area. Around lunchtime, he decided to go back to the Eight Days Inn Restaurant at I-75 for lunch. Upon arriving at the inn, he noticed a young man wolfing down a salad like he was very hungry. He also noticed the young man had water instead of cola like most young people would have. Jeff started eating his lunch but kept an eye on the young man noticing that he had made about three trips to the salad bar and drank two or three glasses of water and thought, *This kid is really hungry*. Jeff felt something was out of place. Before Jeff finished his lunch, the young man had gotten up and left.

When he finished his lunch and left the restaurant, he noticed the silver car sitting down below and alongside the Withlacoochee River bridge again. At which time, he immediately turned around after crossing the bridge. The car had been sitting there for two days. He noticed there was no one fishing when he turned around. His curiosity got the best of him. He remembered a good officer will take a second look at something if it seems out of place. As he pulled in behind the silver Oldsmobile parked at the edge of the river, he noticed it had a Georgia tag. Jeff called the Ridge Manor Dispatch for a 10-28-29, which meant registration check and or stolen check. The stolen check came back that the car was not stolen and was registered to a Mr. Wood in Milledgeville, Georgia. He remembered something from his training and years of experience watching older officers, which he had picked up, and wrote the tag number in his hand, just in case something went wrong. You never know, it could be a bad guy after all. The tag number would be found in his hand so his fellow officers would know where to start looking, if he were unable to speak. He got out of his patrol car to take a look around and eased his way up near the car and carefully walk around the vehicle and found it to be empty. He looked around before proceeding any farther to make sure nobody was around the vehicle. "You can't be too careful," he said later. He then walked down to the riverbank, which was below the car. He noticed a young man sitting in the sandbank on the edge of the river with his head in his hand and staring at the dark water.

Jeff said he spoke to the young fella. "Hey, bud. Are you okay?"

The young man turned around and looked at Jeff and turned back and looked at the river and replied, "Yes, sir. I'm all right."

Jeff said he knew something was troubling the fella. He eased on up and asked to see the young man's identification or his driver's license and asked if the silver car belonged to him. The young fella said to Jeff, "Yes, sir." Jeff then took his license and ran it through

NCIC and FCIC, which came back negative. He was not wanted, and he was given his license back.

As the young man stood up, he faced the sergeant. He could see tears in his eyes and said, "Son, do you need help? What's wrong?"

At this point, Christer Wood said, "Yes, sir, there is," and began to tell the story of how he and his brother had traveled down to Clearwater to try out for a Major League team. He further said his brother made the team, but he did not. He was extremely upset that he would disappoint his family and friends back in Milledgeville that he wasn't good enough to make the team. Jeff said he could see the young man was visibly shaken over this ordeal and felt compassion for the young man, having two young ones that loved baseball. He felt like he wanted to do something to help the young man.

Jeff was a pretty good judge of character and honed those skills over the years and decided to do something he had never done before; he asked the young fella if he wanted to go home with him that afternoon. Christer said he sure would like to. Jeff told him to leave the car there and lock it up, and they would pick it up on the way home that afternoon. Christer told him that it was just about out of gas. Jeff gave him $5 to hold for later that day to buy some gas to get the car to his house.

He took Christer to the substation where they talked in his office. The young man told him that he and his brother had always been competitors and that was why it was so important for him to make the team also, and he did not want to go home to face his family and friends. The sergeant told Christer there was no shame in failure as long as you have done the best you can do. There was always next year, but he could see that the young man's heart was broken. Jeff seemed to have a way with helping people and would always reach out to do what he could to give them a hand up.

Jeff told Christer to follow him home and park his car at his house. They arrived at home about six o'clock that evening. Jeff's wife was fixing supper and was introduced to Christer. His wife asked him to step into the other room. At which time, she asked him who the young man was. After he told her the story, she told Jeff that she trusted his judgment and that he seemed like he was a nice young man.

Around six thirty in the evening, they sat down at the table to have supper after saying grace. The two men talked about the young man's future. Christer seemed to be somewhat cheered up by the hospitality. The young man told them he was from Milledgeville, Georgia, and that his family was middle-class working people and they all had a good family relationship and he had never been in trouble. Jeff already knew this because he had run Christer's name through the computer system and found out he did not have any criminal history. Christer was pleasant and seemed to have a good personality. They enjoyed their dinner and spent the evening chatting in the living room. Jeff could tell he really loved baseball and sports.

The next day, Jeff took Christer to work with him on a ride along after talking to the sheriff and telling him the story at the office in Brooksville. They had a normal day, with only a few minor calls.

That evening, Christer decided it was time to call his dad after discussing it with Jeff during the day. That evening, Jeff made the call to Christer's father in Georgia. Mr. Wood was very happy to hear his son was safe and with someone who was looking after him. Christer asked his father to wire him the money to come home later that week. The arrangements were made, and the young fella was relieved that he had spoken to his dad and he felt comfortable with staying at the Duval's home.

Jeff contacted his two sons, Jeffery and Avery, and told them he had a young man that had tried out for a Major League Baseball team visiting, and they would get to meet him that afternoon. The two boys were excited when they met Christer and stayed huddled around him talking about baseball all afternoon. The three really hit it off great. Christer seemed to be happy again, getting all this attention.

Jeff said they had a get-together out at his property Saturday evening. He said on Saturday morning they went over to the property and cut some firewood and then came back in the evening and lit the fire before dark. They cooked some hot dogs and had a good time. They introduced Christer to some of Jeffery and Avery's baseball friends. The boys' friends started showing up, and they were all excited about meeting this young baseball player. They stayed until late in the night enjoying the fire and talking baseball. A good time was had by all the young men. It must have been around one o'clock in the morning before they all left to go home.

The next morning, Jeffery and Avery were up early and were outside playing with the horse and the dog. Shortly after that, they all had breakfast and kind of milled around the house and enjoyed a quiet Sunday.

Christer received the money Sunday afternoon, and his father was expecting him home by Monday evening. Jeffery and Avery hated to say goodbye. They had really formed a bond with the young man.

The two kids went to school on Monday morning after saying so long to their newfound friend. Later that morning, Jeff walked out to the car with Christer Wood, shook his hand, and wished him good luck and told him not to give up on a dream just because he didn't make it the first time. The young man had tears in his eyes and thanked Jeff for being so kind and helping him. Jeff told Christer to keep his head up. "You have a bright future ahead of you. No matter what you do, you are a smart young man with a great personality. Now hit the road. You don't want to be late. Just be careful." The two said goodbye. Jeff watched him drive away. It was sad to see him go. He wondered what would happen to the young man.

Mr. Wood called that night and said his son was home safe and sound and that Jeff was a real asset to the sheriff's office and thanked him for taking care of his son. Jeff told Mr. Wood there was no thanks necessary. "It's our job to serve and protect the people. That's what I'm here for." The two men said goodbye.

Jeff has wondered for many years what happened to the young baseball player, Christer Wood, but has never heard from him or seen him again.

Some thirty years later, it still haunts Jeff. He wonders what ever became of Christer Wood, the young man who dreamed of being a baseball star.

Jeff's two sons, Jeff II and Avery, played baseball. Jeff played shortstop for FSU. Avery was drafted by the Texas Rangers out of high school, throwing 94 mph.

Jeff and his sons over the years have discussed the story of Christer Wood with fond memories. The boys are now grown, successful businessmen with families, but have never forgotten Christer Wood.

THE MANSFIELD MURDERS

This story begins with a missing girl at a campground west of Brooksville in 1977 or 1978. Jeff relayed the story to me that the fifteen-year-old girl was visiting the campground with her parents and decided to walk down to the Recreation Room.

A young fifteen-year-old girl by the name of Elly Mills was reported missing by her father. Elly had gone to the Rec Room at the KOA while per parents were camping there on Sunday evening, where she was befriended by eighteen-year-old Billy Manville Jr. Witnesses said that Elly and Billy Manville Jr. were seen playing pool for a couple of hours and were seen leaving the KOA Campground together.

Deputy Cliff Batten arrived shortly thereafter to assist Deputy Duval in locating the young girl. A search of the area turned up nothing, and as the sun began to set and it began to get dark, the search was called off for the evening.

The next morning, the sheriff met with Deputy Duval, Det. Cliff Batten, and Capt. John Whitman, with CID, to discuss how to proceed with the case. It was at this time the case was turned over to Captain Whitman so he could head up the investigation. The Sheriff's Posse was notified around noon. An extensive search began of the surrounding area.

Captain Whitman and Detective Batten determined that the young girl, Elly Mills, had befriended Billy Manville Jr. while playing pool in the Rec Room that Sunday evening at the KOA Campground. That was the last time Elly Mills was seen alive.

The following day, Captain Whitman and Detective Batten proceeded to the home of Billy Manville Jr. off Highway 19, on the west side of the county, to question Billy. Upon being questioned, Billy said that he had talked to her but denied leaving the KOA Campground with the girl.

The next day, the search intensified by calling in the search dogs and helicopters. After a week of searching the area, the search came up empty. CID then began to believe Elly Mills had possibly been murdered and was not a simple runaway and began to zero in on the last person to see her alive, Billy Manville Jr.

The state attorney's lead investigator for the Fifth Judicial Circuit, Jimmy Brown, was called into the case to join in on the investigation. The state attorney notified FDLE in Tallahassee of the information they had obtained. The investigators contacted one of the county's circuit judges to try and obtain a search warrant for the Manville residence and property. A few days later, the search warrant was entered by the circuit judge.

FDLE arrived on the scene the next day and began to cordon off the backyard and the residence, thinking Elly Mills might be found at the Manville home.

Captain Whitman, Det. Cliff Batten, and the state attorney's lead investigator, Jimmy Brown, were present at the reading of the search warrant to Billy Manville Sr. at his home. Upon executing the search warrant, it was discovered that eye bolts were screwed into the brick fireplace along with chains. It was later discovered this was how Elly had been chained and kept for a period. Apparently, she was fed while being chained and possibly sexually abused in the house by Billy Manville Sr. and Junior. It was also discovered there was an old green school bus on the property where Elly may have been taken for periods of time and abused and possibly murdered.

When they began to search the outside perimeter of the home, a cadaver dog hit on a spot just below the kitchen sink window. The area was cordoned off, and FDLE began to dig. The body of a young female was discovered in a shallow four-foot grave in the sandy soil. It was not the body of Elly Mills.

Thus, the search continued to other areas of the backyard where three other bodies of young girls were exhumed in shallow graves behind the house.

When the investigators would shut down the search of the property in the evening, off-duty officers, including Jeff Duval, would be posted in the backyard to watch over the open graves to make sure the chain of evidence was protected and no one disturbed or molested the crime scene during the long dark hours of night, as the Manvilles lurked around inside the house at night. It gave Jeff an eerie feeling sitting in the dark behind the house because he could see the killers moving around inside behind the blinds. Occasionally, he would get out of the car to stretch and to let the Manvilles know they were being watched. Every so often, he would peer inside one of the dark holes and smell the stench of death all around him. It would make anyone feel uneasy to be in this kind of atmosphere for twelve hours in the long night knowing the killers could slip out the front of the house and work their way around behind an officer. This heightened the uneasiness. No wonder, after all the years of service and seeing and being involved in cases, officers suffer from PTSD!

Elly Mills' body was discovered among the bodies of three other young girls while executing the search warrant.

A gold wedding band was found in Elly's grave. This information was kept very quiet, and not everyone in the investigative team was privy to this information.

Billy Manville Jr. was arrested and charged by Capt. John Whitman with first-degree murder and booked into the Hernando County Jail. Later on, Jeff said he remembered Billy Manville Sr. was also arrested and charged with accessory to murder. Years later, Captain Whitman told me they really weren't sure who did the killings, but it was a good thing both men were in prison. Billy Manville Sr. died years later while serving time.

Sometime later, California authorities contacted the CID Unit inquiring about a young girl being murdered in California years before, and they knew that the Manvilles had been in the area during that time, and they were aware of the murders in Hernando County and believe the Manvilles were connected to their case.

The California authorities arranged for Billy Manville Jr. to be extradited to Santa Cruz, California, and they charged him with the murder of the young girl.

Jeff told me he personally felt Billy Manville Sr. did the killing in California, and Billy Manville Jr. knew or may have been involved as a younger boy and followed in his father's footsteps. Even a pack of wild young hyenas learn to kill their prey by watching the alpha male kill.

Captain Whitman flew to Santa Cruz to interview the killer. Upon arrival at the airport in Santa Cruz, he was met by two detectives from the Santa Cruz Sheriff's Office. The next morning, Captain Whitman met with the detectives, and after being briefed, he walked into the interview room to interview Billy, along with one of the other detectives. When they sat down at the table, Billy asked if he could have a cigarette. Whitman looked over at the detective and nodded yes. The detective lit a cigarette and gave it to Billy. After Billy's rights were read, they began to discuss the murders in Hernando County.

Whitman looked at Billy and said, "I bet you're surprised to see me."

Billy then took a long, slow drag off the cigarette and blew the smoke over to Whitman and then stated, "Well, if you sons of bitches hadn't found the ring in the grave, you wouldn't be here."

At that time, John Whitman smiled and then replied, "Who said anything about a ring, Billy?"

Billy said, "I know that is how you connected me to the murders in Hernando County. I lost that ring in one of those graves. I know that is how you connected me with the killings in Hernando County. If I hadn't lost that ring, y'all would not have connected me to those murders. If I could have found that damn ring, things would have been a lot different."

As the interview concluded, Captain Whitman felt a sense of achievement. As he turned to walk out of the interview room, Billy stood up and said, "I never thought you guys would find that ring." With this, Captain Whitman smiled and walked out of the room. The door was closed on Billy Manville Jr.

At the time of this writing, Billy Manville Jr. is still serving time in California and has refused to sign extradition back to Hernando County, Florida. Capt. John Whitman was enjoying his retirement in the hills of ole Kentucky with his significant other, a beautiful, sweet lady, who loved him very much.

This story is dedicated to the memory of Capt. Johnny Lee Whitman and Det. Cliff Batten of the Hernando County Sheriff's Office.

BIG GAME WARDEN "RONNIE"

This story is about a one-of-a-kind lawman. The man stood six feet and five and a half inches. Ronnie was big in stature and strong as an ox. He had black hair and dark eyes that were full of mischief. Ronnie was always up to some kind of funny mischief. Problem was, he didn't understand just how strong he was.

Jeff met Ronnie long about 1960. His mother worked at Weeki Wachee Springs at the time and so did Ronnie's beautiful wife, Jean Ann. My mother Jackie and Jean Ann worked together at Weeki Wachee for several years. Man, she was a looker! Jeff first saw the big man at the Springs Christmas Party and asked his mother who the pretty girl was.

She said, "You see the huge man standing by her?"

Jeff replied, "Yep."

His mother said, "That's Ronnie and his wife. I work with her here at the Springs."

Well at the time, Jeff was a thirteen-year-old boy with big eyes admiring all the pretty mermaids walking around the party. No way was this kid going to look twice at the giant's girl.

Several years later, one evening, Jeff and a couple of his buddies got a six pack of Bud and drove out to the lake north of town. Just before getting to the lake turnoff, a big red light came on behind them. Jeff looked in the outside mirror and saw the big man unfolding out of his car and thought, *Dang, we're busted! Big Ronnie, game warden, got us!*

He walked up and said, "What you boys doing?" while shining that big flashlight on the six-pack of Bud and smiling.

Jeff was thinking, *Man, anybody but him. He's friends with Mom. I'm in big trouble!*

Ronnie said, "Step out of the car."

Jeff replied, "Ronnie, sir, the beer is mine and it's unopened, sir."

"Yeah, I see you're not drinkin', are you?"

Jeff answered, "No, sir."

"I'm gonna take this beer. You boys go home."

He knew Jeff's mom's car. They drove back to Brooksville and was relieved not to be arrested. He knew good and well Ronnie was going to enjoy their beer at some point!

Retired Sheriff Jamie Adams once told Jeff when he was hired into the Fish and Game as a warden, Big Ronnie was his training officer. Now, Ronnie was a good warden. However, he loved to pull pranks on everybody.

Sheriff Adams told Jeff Ronnie was getting into his patrol car at a service station up town, and while trying to get in, he put his big hand on a grenade-loaded gas shotgun. Somehow, he blew a hole in the transmission of his car. The gas station was abandoned for an hour while the tear-gas was smoking. It looked like the game warden's car was on fire! Brother what a hoot. The fire department came rushing up and then rushed right back out when they got gassed, along with the city police in Brooksville!

In 1970, Jeff was working in the radio room. He said he saw Ronnie pull up in front of the sheriff's office in Brooksville. Two other deputies were standing just inside the door at the old sheriff's office and county jail. Jeff said when the big game warden got out of his car, he was holding a four-foot gator under his arm. Jeff knew what was a fixin' to happen, so he ran behind the first barred door and locked it, not saying anything to the only colored deputies in Hernando County. Ole Jeff loved these two men like brothers but just could not miss the fun.

Now, picture this going down. Big Ronnie came in the front door, the gator hanging straight down under his left arm, never saying a word, just grinning that grin. When he got to the end of the front counter, he tossed the gator on the counter. The two deputies were drinkin' some jailhouse coffee on the counter. Now total chaos broke loose, chaos and pandemonium. It was like watching a slapstick movie. Ole Ronnie was jumping around the small radio room, slapping his knee, laughing, while the other buddies were screaming and about to tear the old wooden windowed door off at the hinges while pulling each other backward trying to get out of the gator's way. That gator was growling and slapping his tail and slinging his head wildly on the counter. His tail teed off one heavy cup of coffee right through a front windowpane. He thought Ronnie was going to die laughing and shouting, "Damn, that's a hole in one!"

Jeff ran out the door. The gator had the front office. As he ran out, Ronnie and the gator were both laughing, he thought! Jeff was looking down Jefferson Street and saw the other two deputies turn the corner onto Bell Avenue, still screaming and yelling. He wasn't too far behind them. Then he realized, no one was running the ship and walked back up to the front porch, looked inside, and saw the giant game warden drinking coffee and the gator lying on the floor. Ronnie was tossing him light bread and was telling that alligator how they had run the deputies down the road!

Jeff told me they had asked the big man to assist in a drug raid one night down around Weeki Wachee Woodlands. When the deputy went in the front door, the huge game warden just stood on the back porch like a goalie playing in a championship game, standing bent over with his arms out. When those boys saw him, they ran back inside and gave up.

Jamie Adams said they went out one night together and picked a back seat full of muskmelons and then drove to the airport, south of town. Ronnie was driving a '68 Dodge big block. Jamie said they drove down the runway about 140 mph. The big man would tell Jamie to let a muskmelon go easy. The muskmelons would roll so fast ahead of them and would start jumping up about forty feet and explode. Just having fun back in the day!

Jeff told me one Sunday morning he was patrolling out around McKethan Lake real early and saw a man sleeping on the edge of the lake. He said he drove down to check the car and driver out, and about the time he got near the suspicious car, he saw a man jump out screaming and slinging his arms around and doing a high step away from the car. When Jeff got close to the fracas, he saw the man trying to sling two possums off his shoulder. The man had gotten drunk and parked off the road. When Jeff saw the car full of possums, he knew the big game warden had struck again.

After about eighteen years in the area, the major in Tallahassee decided to let another county share in all this fun. Ronnie was transferred up around Alachua County where the big man was born and raised. Jeff said most people really liked Ronnie and missed his antics when he left the area. Somehow, Jeff said everybody in Fish and Game in Florida knew stories they liked to share about the big game warden.

Jeff and I sat and remembered other stories. One was about when he transferred to Gulf County, Florida, where his roots grew deep in the soil of Florida. He said he had become friends with another ole Florida boy in North Gulf County, Otis Davis. He was a deputy sheriff who lived in Wewahitchka, along the Apalachicola River, which is also known as the Big River. He went on to say that he and Otis had become friends quickly. They had a lot in common. Ole Otis loved to prank people too. He had light hair and blue eyes and stood about average height and had a little sideways grin and a twinkle in his eyes. Otis's wife and kids quickly adopted Jeff. Jeff said they became family. Besides, Mrs. Deb made some of the best buttermilk biscuits in the country!

The first time Jeff saw Otis Davis, he was picking up his two girls at school in his old red Ford pickup. The kids were gathering around the truck, Jeff noticed, and had to know what this fellow had in that cage in the back of his truck.

When he drove up and got out, Jeff asked, "What do you have in the cage bud?"

The man grinned with a mischievous look and said in a real Southern drawl, "A wildcat."

Well, their friendship grew from there. Otis and his kids became family. The two were always scheming something up.

One night, they slipped upon the chief of Police in Wewa and tied a bra to the end of his eighteen-inch antenna. About two hours later, the chief pulled in the Dixie Dandy. Everyone in the parking lot was laughin' and pointing at the pretty pink bra, except Otis and Jeff. The chief walked over to the deputies and said, "Y'all know who might have pulled this one?" The two deputies just shook their heads no.

Jeff said he loved the Davis family. He had been introduced to Otis's mom and dad who lived across the field. They were great people. Jeff's first Christmas back in the panhandle, he was single and living alone. The Davis family invited him over Christmas Eve for a family get-together in Wewa. They sang Christmas carols around the ole family piano. He then met Otis's brother-in-law, Jimmy Williams, who was also the chief deputy at the Franklin County Sheriff's Office. He and Jimmy formed a friendship also. The Davis family made him feel so much at home and welcome. He really felt he was part of their family and will always love them.

After Jeff retired, he moved back down to Central Florida. He often remembered Otis and some of the things, like the day Otis asked him if he liked to fish. Jeff told him he did. When they got out on the river, unbeknownst to Jeff, Otis pulled out a stick of dynamite. Otis lit it while Jeff was turned around casting his line out. Jeff said he heard something hit the water and thought Otis had cast a plug out. All of a sudden, the river seemed to rise up and shake, spitting up all kinds of fish, eels, and mud. Jeff was tossed backward and hit the bottom of the flatboat and said, "Damn, Otis, what happened?" as fish, all kinds and sizes, were landing in the boat, around them.

Jeff said he looked up at ole Otis and saw him grin that little grin and said, "You wanted to go fishing. Now let's net them quick and get gone."

Jeff asked, "Do you know they will lock us both up if a game man comes up?"

Otis replied, "Naw." Jeff never asked Otis to go fishing again but wondered what he did hunt with.

*****

Did y'all notice how I segue way this story about ole Otis into the game warden story? That's a new word I heard the other day and just had to use it. This story is dedicated to the Otis Davis family.

FREDDIE THE FREELOADER (A.K.A. DOC TANYA)

Jeff said he met Freddie the Freeloader, as he called him. His real name was Freddie Williamson. Freddie in Jeff's opinion was doing life on the installment plan in the Hernando County Jail. Freddie was known around town for being a simpleminded wino and thief. Jeff said he always felt ole Freddie would wind up dead in a ditch in the last of his days.

When one of the deputies or city police officers would spot Freddie on the street somewhere, he would suddenly become "Doc Tanya" as he would snap to attention and salute the officers and do a little jump back and point his fingers straight to the heavens and shout out loud, "Doc Tanya is on the line," while tipping his hat and bowing to the officers.

Most of the officers would drive on by with a smile, but Jeff would sometimes take the time to stop and talk to Doc Tanya. He said you usually could smell the Mad Dog 20/20 when you rolled your window down. Freddie usually had a *Playboy Magazine* rolled up under his arm and would have to show you some pictures of the girls in the magazine. Jeff usually would ask him where he found those magazines, knowing they probably fell into his pocket as he walked by the girlie magazine rack, and he just left them there.

Now ole Doc always had a hiding place for his magazines and jug of wine. One day while out and about, Jeff was sitting on the side of the road with a pair of binoculars. When he saw Freddie coming up the road wearing his funny little hat, he suddenly stopped at a corner near a wooded lot, jumped down the culvert, jerked out his girly magazine and his jug of Mad Dog 20/20, and began gettin' on down the road, as "Doc" would say, with the magazine rolled up under his arm and the bottle of wine in his back pocket. Jeff said he just drove off and never told Freddie until about two years later what he had seen.

When confronted with the story, ole Freddie, a.k.a. Doc Tanya, roared back and laughed. "Yes, sir, Mr. Jeff, you got to hide your wine and your women 'cause if you don't, somebody gonna want to try a little bit of both of them."

Jeff couldn't help but laugh out loud. He said, "I declare, Doc, you're probably right about that."

The city police really loved to pick ole Freddie up. They were always getting him for public intoxication. The ole county judge, Monroe Freeman, might give ole Freddie thirty days in the county jail for a minor offense. For a more serious charge, like picking up things that didn't belong to him, he would sentence ole Freddie up to six months in the county jail. Freddie didn't really mind. He always had friends like ole Howg Head, Shootem Up, or Ole Blue in there to kill time with; and he was always made a trustee by the sheriff, who might just need a little carpentry work done around the jail. You see, Freddie was a master carpenter. He once told Jeff he had learned the trade from his daddy as soon as he was old enough to swing a hammer. He also did paintin' around the jail and the sheriff's office. He was quite a handy man.

In the early years of 1968 and 1969, Jeff worked in the office as a dispatcher and corrections officer and got to know Freddie very well as the two had become friends. Jeff said he spent as much time at the sheriff's office as he did at home working seventy-two hours per week for a whopping $350 per month. "How could you not love such a job?" he once stated.

Now, back to Doc Tanya or Freddie the Freeloader. One morning while working the desk, he saw the county judge walking up the sidewalk toward the sheriff's office. He couldn't help but notice the judge's ever-present blue bow tie when the judge came through the door. Jeff knew something was wrong. The judge had that look on his face.

Jeff said, "Good morning, Judge."

The judge did not respond with a nicety. The judge looked Jeff in the face with a scowl and said, "I'm ordering Freddie Williamson to be arrested right now."

Jeff wanted to respond so bad by saying, "Well, Judge, do you have a warrant?" but he knew Monroe was not in a joking mood. "Yes, sir Judge. What has he done now?"

The judge replied, "He stole a gun out of my house while he was over there doing some paintwork."

Again, Jeff wanted to come back with a funny remark like, "Well, Judge, did you hire a thief?" but knew better and choked it back. It seemed as though Freddie helped himself to the judge's pistol while the judge wasn't looking.

After being arrested, ole Doc confessed. The judge's pistol was recovered, and the judge gave ole Freddie the coup de grâce, eleven months and twenty-nine days in the Hernando County Jail. Many of the town's folks got a little laugh out of the judge hiring a known thief to work around their house.

Jeff liked the ole judge. They had many conversations while Jeff was his bailiff during trials. He was a true Southern gentleman. Jeff was kind of saddened after thirty years on the bench, the judge finally had to run for reelection. He was defeated by a donut maker from out of town. Jeff thought about running for county judge himself and thought he could win by a landslide with his experience as a law enforcement officer but couldn't find it in his heart to run against his ole friend, Monroe Freeman.

After Freddie's sentencing, Jeff said he asked him, "Why in the world did you think you could get away with stealing the judge's gun?"

His reply was "I was on that ole mad dog and thought I could sell the gun and get some more wine."

One evening after everyone left the office, Freddie was cleaning up the kitchen, and when he got through, he came to dispatch and sat down to rest before going back to his sleeping quarters. Jeff said he told him eleven months and twenty-nine days was going to be a long stay. At which time, ole Freddie smiled and said, "Mr. Jeff, I get my Social Security check every month while I'm in jail, and I put that in the bank, and with the money I get from shinin' everybody's boots, and then when I get out in a year, I will have some money in the bank."

Jeff said he knew right then ole Doc Tanya was not just a crazy ole wino.

Now talking about shining shoes, ole Doc Tanya was one of the best shoe-shining, rag-popping, spit-shining men he had ever seen. He put that polish on with his fingers and took that rag and put a mirror shine on a pair of boots. Jeff said he always gave him a little extra because Freddie was a friend and not just another inmate.

He said when he retired in the mid-1990s in Gulf County and came back to Brooksville, one of the first people he thought of was ole Freddie "Doc Tanya" Williamson himself. He said he kept an eye open around town but never saw ole Freddie anywhere and feared he may have died in the nine years he was out of the county. That's when he decided to go see another old friend, Mr. Joe Black Walker, who had been his friend for most of his life. Joe knew everybody on the south side of town. When he met with Joe Walker, he was advised that ole Doc was doing great. Jeff said he was taken back for a few moments after hearing that statement.

Jeff asked Joe, "How is he doing, Joe?"

Joe said, "Fine."

Jeff told Joe, "I haven't been able to find him anywhere. He's usually loafing around town with that jug of Mad Dog 20/20 or in jail."

Much to Jeff's surprise, Joe said, "He's in a rest home out at Lake Lindsey."

The two men decided to go right then to visit Doc Tanya, ole Freddie. Upon arriving at the rest home, they saw their old friend, Freddie, raking leaves in the front yard of the rest home, just like he had done many years before at the ole county sheriff's office in downtown Brooksville.

As Jeff walked around the front of Joe's car, he yelled, "Hey, Doc. What are you doing?"

Ole Freddie froze upon hearing his old friend's voice. He did the jump back, saluted, and stood straight up with his hands pointing to the sky, like he had done a thousand times before, and said, "Doc Tanya is on the line. Mr. Jeff, is that you?"

Jeff replied, "It sho' is, Freddie."

Freddie ran and gave his old friend a big hug and said, "Lord have mercy. Mr. Jeff, where in the world have you been so long?"

Jeff told him he had transferred to Gulf County as third in command in 1988 and was there about nine years, but often thought about his old friend Freddie. Joe joined in laughing and slapping his knee and said, "Lord if I didn't know better, I would think y'all were kinfolks."

Freddie told Jeff he had found the Lord and didn't want any more Mad Dog and didn't even want to go to town and steal nothing or get into trouble. He said, "I'm a new man." Jeff felt a tear run down his cheek. He was overjoyed that ole Doc Tanya had finally seen the light and seemed to be so happy.

Ole Freddie said, "Y'all come in. I want to show you my room. I love it so much here, out in the country." Freddie showed Joe and Jeff his room and his meager trinkets he had in his one-bedroom apartment. They visited for about an hour, and they reminisced about the old times when they were much younger. Joe and Jeff drove back to Brooksville after telling Freddie goodbye and that he would see him in a few weeks.

About a month later, one evening, the phone rang at Jeff's home. It was his friend Joe Walker. Joe said, "Jeff, I got some bad news. I just found out that Freddie Williamson, ole Doc, has gone home to be with the Lord. The family has asked that you give a eulogy for our old friend, Doc Tanya."

At which time, Jeff replied, "It would be an honor." The day of the funeral service, the church was crowded with family and friends. Jeff said as he was walking up to the front of the church, he looked at Doc lying there peacefully, and he remembered so many years ago thinking that his friend would die drunk down along the roadside alone. Jeff realized miracles do happen and truly believed ole Freddie was in heaven with his Lord. He couldn't help but wonder, when he walked through the pearly gate, if he saluted, did the jump back step, pointed straight up, and shouted, “Praise ye Lord. Doc Tanya is on the line.”

BILLY BOB RIDES INTO TOWN

. . . .

One Saturday around noon, a local cowboy who enjoys his beer came riding into downtown Brooksville on his horse.

The city police only had one officer on duty that day, Big Scott, a friend of Jeff's. The sheriff's office had two men on duty, Jeff and Billy Donn, who was working the west side of the county.

Jeff was out patrolling the county and heard the call go out to Big Scott—Billy Bob was riding into town on his horse and was three sheets in the wind. Jeff knew where Billy Bob's favorite bar was, Johnny's Bar and Pool Hall on Main Street. Jeff decided to park on the corner of Main Street and Broad Street and wait for all the fun to begin.

Billy Bob, wearing his cowboy hat, came riding into town on his horse right up Main Street. Dang, it sure was a funny sight! Billy Bob road that dang horse right up inside Johnny's Bar. He ordered a beer for himself and four in a bucket for his horse, ole Reb. Now, Johnny served up the beer without argument because Billy Bob could get a little mean if he was drinking.

Johnny called the city police to let them know that Billy Bob was drunk and had ridden his horse right into his bar and didn't know which one was the drunkest, ole Reb or Billy Bob. Jeff watched as Big Scott pulled up to the bar and went in.

Now, Big Scott was a short heavy-built fella. All of a sudden, Big Scott came running out the door with ole Reb right behind him, just a buckin', and Billy Bob looking like a bronc rider, chasing Big Scott down the street toward the courthouse. Jeff was really enjoying the show! Big Scott was just ahead of the drunk horse and the cowboy was doing his best to try and hang on. It was the funniest thing Jeff had ever seen. He was laughing so hard that he was crying.

When they all got to the corner of Jefferson Street and Main Street, next to the bank, a little gray-haired lady was standing there with her umbrella in her hand. Big Scott was trying to pull Billy Bob off ole Reb, who was spinning and raring up. About this time, the little old lady slapped ole Reb on the rump with her umbrella. Ole Reb jumped right out into the middle of Jefferson Street, doing a four-legged split. Jeff had to rush to assist Big Scott since they all were lying in the middle of Jefferson Street before someone got hurt.

Big Scott was worn out and said, "Man, I am sure glad you showed up." He didn't know that Jeff had been there the entire time watching all the fun. Jeff called the Range Riders to pick up the drunk horse and lock him up.

It was the only time a drunk horse and a drunk cowboy had ever been arrested in Hernando County at the same time.

It was even funnier than the day that the gorilla got loose from the circus in Inverness. I would have liked to have seen that show too. Can you imagine a gorilla running around town with a bunch of lawmen chasing him? They finally darted and sedated the big fella and took him back to his cage. Man, what a hoot!

ANDY AND THE "HE COON"

Andy was one of the first black deputy sheriffs in Hernando County in the mid to late 1960s. I worked with him and two other black officers in the early days of my career. They were all good men and good officers. I enjoyed their company, and we were all good friends; we did like to have fun!

Now Andy did like his women. Sometimes after two o'clock in the morning on Friday and Saturday nights, when the drunks and crazies went home, Andy would ask to ride with me. We would ride till daylight talking about them gals and having a laugh.

Now, ole Andy told me a story one evening about one of his ole gals. Sometimes he would leave home saying he had to work an extra detail. He was supposed to get off this extra detail about five o'clock the next morning and go home. Things were just going good on this extra detail for him to leave sweet Essie Mae's arms. Along about daylight, he realized he had overstayed his time. So he slipped out the back door along the alley, setting on a stoop putting his boots on. It was just daylight enough to see up the alley.

All of a sudden, he heard a very familiar voice, yelling, "Heyyyyyy, Andy! Andy, I see you! I see you, Andy!" And with that ole Andy was gone like a streak of white lightning, which would be hard for him to do. He went on home like he would on a regular schedule. His wife was already there. He thought he would have breakfast, but she said to Andy while standing in the kitchen, "Andy, I caught you this morning. I done caught you."

Now ole Andy gave her a strange look, trying to look surprised, and said, "What you mean, woman?"

She said, "I mean I caught you coming out of Essie Mae's back stoop about daylight this morning."

At which time, he said, "You ain't caught me coming out of nothing."

She said, "Yes, I did. I saw you."

Andy asked, "Did you catch me, really? When you catch me, you slap me on my butt and tell me to get up. Until you do that, you ain't caught Andy doing nothing."

She went on and fixed Andy's breakfast and didn't speak another word all day. She knew Andy knowed how he was and accepted that. Nothing more was ever said about this matter.

One full moon night, Andy and I were out on Seminole Road, easing along in the cool night air and a big "he-coon" ran out in front of us. We hit that coon and killed him dead, right there. Andy put in on me to go back and get that coon.

At which time, I said, "No! What do you want with that big coon?"

His reply was, "Barbeque coon is mighty good eating."

Now, I had tried baked coon before and didn't care for it, and besides I was always mister neat and clean and always kept my patrol car spotless and couldn't imagine that bloody coon in my patrol car floorboard. Andy kept on and I couldn't turn my friend down, so we returned to the scene. Andy got out and picked that "he-coon" up, and then he opened the back door and chucked it in behind me. We then drove off and forgot about the coon.

We started laughing and talking about his gals again. Then all of a sudden, Andy screamed, "He ain't dead! He ain't dead!" That coon started under my seat growling and clawing at my butt. "Stop. He ain't dead! Stop. He ain't dead!" I knew this cracker was gonna let Andy and that "he-bull coon" have that damn patrol car.

We ran off the road down into a ditch and through a fence. I jumped out and ran as hard as I could run to get away from that big coon. Then I heard shots and stopped, looked back, and realized that Andy was shooting bullet holes in my brand-new Dodge patrol car, as that coon was trying to escape, and Andy was cussing that wild-ass coon.

Even though it took me a week to get the smell of the coon poop out of my car, I don't think the high sheriff believed the story of how my car got shot up. He may have thought it was some "good ole boy" after me, but it wasn't!

Several years later, Andy had a major stroke, and they put him into a nursing home. As soon as I found out about his stroke, I knew that I had to go visit him. I went over to visit him at the nursing home one afternoon, and when I saw him lying there, I knew that he wouldn't be going home. When I walked over to his bedside, he looked up at me and smiled. He could hardly speak. I asked him if there was anything I could do for him. After a little while, he smiled again and was able to say, "I sure would like some Oreo cookies and milk." I knew that he probably wasn't supposed to have them but decided that I would get them for him anyway. I went to a nearby store and bought the milk and cookies and brought them back to my dear old friend Andy. I knew that he would have done the same for me.

As I walked back up to his bed, he said, "I knowed you'd come back with me some milk and cookies." I stayed a few more minutes, but I realized as I was leaving that I would probably never see my old friend again.

I was out of town when Andy passed away, working in Gulf County. When I came back to Brooksville, I drove out to his grave and thought about all the times we had spent together. As I stood in the cemetery alone looking at my dear old friend's grave, my heart began to feel heavy knowing we would never laugh together again. I felt the warm tears running down my cheek while I was reminiscing about my dear friend. I knew if he would talk to me, he would say, "Don't worry about ole Andy 'cause I had time enough to get my life right before I was called home, Jeff."

I began to remember the ole saying, "Old lawmen never die. They just go to heaven and regroup." We had a lot of fun but were always professional when it came to doing our job. I have thought of him often as the years have rolled by.

A few years later, I was fortunate enough to train a new young black recruit, Floyd Moore, who was the third African-America to be hired by Hernando County and a close friend of Andy's. In those years, things were still somewhat segregated but were beginning to change, and I was happy to see those changes coming about. Floyd was a big man, six feet, five inches and about 245 pounds.

Someone once told me that Floyd had a bigger brother that was playing in the NFL and was even bigger than Floyd. I later met his brother. He was a great guy and had played with the Miami Dolphins for several years.

Now Floyd was a little timid because his momma had raised them by herself. She made sure that they were well mannered and that they had a good education, including a college degree. They were raised the old-fashioned way.

This story is dedicated to the first four black deputies to work for the Hernando County Sheriff's Office, Willie Brookens, Andrew Lawsons, Big Jim, and Floyd Moore.

OLE BLUE

Now Ole Blue wasn't just any ole wino. He had a good heart! He just had two things in life that he liked, a blues harmonica and a bottle of Mad Dog 20/20.

He was a little man, so dark that he looked blue, thus the nickname "Ole Blue." Ole Blue is what all his other drinking buddies called him—guys like Howg Head, Doc, Blind Willie, and Shootem' Up!

Now Blind Willie and Shootem' Up were his closest friends. They would get their checks at the end of the month and get on that ole Mad Dog, and then they all would be picked up by the city police and locked up. The next morning, you would hear Ole Blue playing the old blues harmonica all over the jail.

Ron, one of the jailers, would go back and check to see who wanted the bail bondsman. Blue always jumped up and said, "Yesa, I sho' do. Call Mr. Rambie to gets Ole Blue out!"

Ron would ask Blue to play something on that harmonica. Blue would play and dance around and sing. Blue would always ask Ron, "Anything special you want to hear?" He was surely one of the last of the ole natural-born, self-taught, old blues men.

Everybody loved Blue. He was just a sweet, kindly old man who was good to everyone. He really was one of the best blues players you ever would see. He looked like a hobo wearing his old coat, worn-out brogan shoes, and with that paper-wrapped jug of Mad Dog 20/20 in his coat pocket. He was one of a kind.

It's funny how some people have stood out all these years later in my mind, but I really liked this kindly ole hobo. Ole Blue would tell you, with a big toothless smile on his face, he was a hobo. That was just Ole Blue.

One Sunday morning about daylight, Blue and Shootem' Up had been drinking all night. Witnesses said they were standing outside the Blue Flame Juke Joint. Ole Blue had a small amount of Mad Dog 20/20 left for later that day. Shootem' Up wanted that last bit and Blue refused to give it up. That's when his friend pulled a knife and stuck it into Ole Blue's chest. Blue fell to the ground and was heard to say, "You done killed Ole Blue."

Shootem' Up got life in the state prison for killing Ole Blue.

I pray God had mercy on my friend, Ole Blue.

SOUTH OF THE BORDER

....

Now, ole Andy, as you now know, was a funny fellow!

One night, he was riding with me and told me this funny little story. It seems Andy and Willie Brookens decided to go to Mexico. At the time, Andy had a 1965 Volkswagen Bug, just the thing to take on a long trip.

Andy said they were doing good and enjoying the trip westward from Brooksville. Once they got to Texas, they stopped for a rest and spent a day or two in San Antonio, just having a great time.

Ole Andy said going through the border check was a little tense, but he got that bug down into Mexico and into the interior of Mexico. Things got a little more difficult, because neither man knew how to speak Spanish. A lot of gesturing was done. I bet that was a hoot. Andy said a few people spoke a little English, but not much though.

I think Willie Bee had to keep an eye on ole Andy, with the troublemaker befriending Andy, that being Jose Cuervo himself. Andy said when he was a young fellow, Jose would get him into a lot of trouble every time, usually over a pretty gal. He would tell me things like, "Go get the pretty girl and dance." Sometimes her boyfriend said no. Jose would say, "Knock him out, dude," and then the fun would begin. Andy, Jose, and the boyfriend would be dancing around the floor with no music, and a crowd would be cheering them on. Anyway, I didn't like dancing with men. I learned a hard lesson and told Jose, "You ain't my friend, brother. Lesson learned."

Now, back to Andy and Willie Bee. They said they found a little Cantina and the girls were nice. The girls loved the tips from these two fellers, and so the fellers got a little extra service. Wooya!

Andy was getting tired, and too much of a good thing can be tiring, you know. So the two decided to retire for the night to their room. It was then ole Andy said he couldn't go to sleep. Willie asked him why and Andy said one of the funniest things I've ever heard. Andy said he told Willie Bee, "You know, Willie, six of them little fellers can tote that little bug off."

Anyway, the next morning, he said that they got up and started looking around this little Mexican town and buying some souvenirs to take home to their family and friends. They enjoyed the trip according to Andy, and the best part of it after all was crossing back into the good old United States, and they didn't lose the bug.

THE LEGEND OF WILLIE POST

The stories of Willie Post were shared by an old friend of Willie's, Jeff Duval, retired sheriff's lieutenant. He said he came to know Willie about 1968, at a time when the country was in turmoil because of the Vietnam War. He said they met on a detail they were working on with the Pasco County Sheriff's Office at Saint Leo College in San Antonio, Florida. It was a joint mission to assist the federal government to aid the Secretary of Defense, Melvin Laird, who was flying in accompanied by the actor Lee Marvin, who had graduated from Saint Leo College.

The reason for them being there was to keep the hippies and "flower children" at a distance since protesters can be violent sometimes toward government officials.

Now getting back to Willie. Willie Post was different from anyone you ever met. Old-school lawman. Willie was born, some people said, in Hillsborough County. It was rumored his father was a well-known wealthy man, but Willie never spoke of his mother and father's family, only of his wife and children, so everyone just left it alone. He appeared to be possibly of Mexican descent; however, Jeff just was not sure. At least that was what Willie wanted everybody to think. He was married to a beautiful Mexican woman, and he spoke fluent Spanish. Willie was about five feet, eight inches, stocky build, with black hair, combed straight back with what appeared to be lard. He always wore black trousers and wore shirts like Al Capone and some others of that era, with a red tie and a pair of sharp pointed Mexican cowboy boots. When Willie walked, he was on a mission, his head cocked back, moving right along, and his bowed legs wobbling down the road. He was a sight to behold.

Jeff said he believed Willie enjoyed working around the migrant labor camps in the late 1960s, because all the Hispanic people identified with him. He would speak fluent Spanish. He had a natural rapport with the Mexican people, and most of them seemed to like Willie.

Willie was employed by the Pasco County Sheriff's Office in the mid-1960s. Everybody would know his voice when it came on the radio, because he had a high-pitched voice, and when you heard, "16 Dade City open the back gate," you knew he was bringing somebody to the Pasco County Jail. Willie was a mess, but everybody seemed to love ole Willie.

In the early 1970s, Pasco County elected a new sheriff. Like so many other deputies all over Florida, it was time for a move. Willie was loyal to the sheriff that he worked for and politicked heavy for him and knew he could not stay in Pasco County any longer.

He came to work in Hernando County in the early 1970s for Sheriff Melvin Kelly, who was a new sheriff at the time. He had hired Willie because he knew of his reputation for being a good law enforcement officer and being able to work with the migrants, which was a plus for the Hernando County Sheriff's Office, since they did not have anyone who spoke fluent Spanish.

Sheriff Kelly decided to put Willie with Sgt. Jeff Duval for a couple of weeks so he could help him become familiar with the county roads, trouble spots, etc.

They would be working the night shift where things were usually slower. Jeff learned a lot from Willie since he was not your typical deputy sheriff as far as his modus operandi when solving a crime or going after a bad guy.

One night when they were working, they began talking. Now Jeff knew Willie was a little different. During the night, Willie said something that rang a bell. He said, "If people in general are even a suspect in a crime and think you are a little crazy, sometimes they will tell you a lot more." He would occasionally let things slip out about his MO when they were alone on patrol. "If a bad guy thinks you're not too smart, and you let him think he is smarter than you and that he can outfox you, that's what you want him to think. He will tell you things unintentionally that you can pick up on." Jeff knew Willie was smart like a fox.

Back in the 1970s and early 1980s, the sheriff's office would let you lease a car of your choice since all the county cars did not have to be marked at that time. Now ole Willie always drove, as long as Jeff knew him, a black Ford four-doors sedan. That was one of his trademarks.

One afternoon about four o'clock, Jeff and some of the other deputies were changing shifts. They were standing on the old colonial porch of the sheriff's office on Jefferson Street. Willie Post drove up and pulled in the circle driveway right in front of the steps with his brand-new black Ford sedan that he had leased that morning. As he stepped out with a grin on his large round face, he said, "Look, guys, I got my new sedan." They all started looking over the car, and Jeff noticed it had rubber floor mats and asked Willie why he didn't get carpet.

Willie rolled his head back and let out a loud laugh and said, "I don't like to spread germs spitting my tobacco out the window."

Everyone looked puzzled. Jeff said, "Where do you spit, in a can?"

At which time Willie laughed again and said, "Open the front driver's door."

The men began to look inside and saw about two inches of black dirt in the front floorboard on the driver's side. Jeff said, "You've got to be kidding me, Willie. You really spit in the floor?"

Willie chuckled and said, "Yeah! I shovel it out about once a week and then put clean dirt in there."

With this, the whole crowd roared. That was just one of the things Jeff learned about his funny friend Willie.

While in Pasco County, Willie used to frequent the 41 Truck Stop in Land O' Lakes. It was a big truck stop. Willie had a couple of CIs that worked there. He got a lot of good information hanging around that truck stop. One morning about one thirty, Willie said, "Jeff, do y'all have a truck stop in Hernando County?"

Jeff replied, "Yes, we do, Willie, but it's a small truck stop up 98 North, near the Rock Mines."

Willie said then, "Let's go get a cup of coffee and check it out."

Little did Jeff know what a show he was about to see.

They arrived at the truck stop about two o'clock in the morning. There were two semis sitting in the parking lot, and the two drivers were inside eating and drinking coffee. When they sat down, Willie said, "See, you are like every other law enforcement officer. You don't sit with your back to the door."

Jeff replied, "That's right, but I have your back, Willie." The young lady came over to take their order. Jeff said, "I will just have coffee."

Willie looked at the waitress and smiled. Jeff knew something was going to happen by the look on Willie's face. He said, "Yes, ma'am. Bring me a six-ounce hot Coca-Cola, a large tea glass, and a cup of strong black coffee."

The waitress didn't know if he was joking or not. She said, "Is that what you really want to drink?"

He said, "Yes, ma'am."

She asked, "Would you like anything to eat?"

Willie said, "Yes, ma'am, I would. Put me a dozen chicken gizzards in a pot of water with lots of black pepper. When they start to boil good, turn them off and bring them to me with some white soda crackers and hot sauce."

The poor girl looked bewildered and said, "Are you serious?"

At which time, Willie said, "Yes, ma'am, I am."

Jeff couldn't help but notice the two truck drivers sitting behind Willie was about to bust to keep from laughing, especially when Willie told the girl to bring him a large tea glass, hot Coke, and hot coffee. He poured them together in the large tea glass and then drank the mixture after stirring it up. Jeff was dumbfounded to see such a concoction being consumed.

Jeff asked, "What in the world is that supposed to be?"

Willie said, "It keeps me awake and alert for twenty-four hours, and as long as I drink this, I can stay awake for a week. It was a truck driver's coffee."

Jeff noticed the truck drivers were about to bust trying not to laugh at Willie's crazy concoction, but they knew better than to laugh at a deputy sheriff in a truck stop. Jeff just sat in dismay and shook his head as Willie Post consumed the chicken gizzards and the "truck driver's coffee." As the two deputies started out the door, Jeff could hear the truck drivers and the waitress laughing loudly as they made their way back to the patrol car.

Lots of truck drivers knew Willie from hanging around the 41 Truck Stop in Land O' Lakes. They liked Willie and knew him well. Everybody liked Willie, except the bad guys.

Willie Post was a legend in Florida law enforcement circles. Jeff soon learned some of his tricks of the trade. Willie Post always had at least three different sets of clothes and shoes in his trunk or as he called them his getups. One was Willie the wino, the traveling hobo, and the sharp-dressed Mexican. Willie always kept his getups in the trunk, along with a bottle of Mad Dog 20/20, wrapped in a paper sack along with an old pair of brogan shoes. When he was Willie the wino and the traveling hobo, he always wore an old felt hat.

When he got ready to be Willie the wino, he always took a swig and rolled it around in his mouth and poured some on his chest. He could be anybody he wanted to be. Sometimes Jeff would even forget who he was once he got into a character, but it was fun to watch him work.

Jeff said he remembered one cold frosty morning they worked a stolen car from the Chevrolet Dealership. Willie called Jeff to meet him at the county sheriff's office. When he arrived, Willie said, "Let's step outside." He advised Jeff of the theft. The two began to plan how to work the case. Willie had information from a confidential informant that a migrant citrus worker had stolen the car. The two teamed up. Willie began to put on his Willie the wino getup. He could not believe what he saw when Willie came stumbling out of the sheriff's office, wearing a pair of overalls, old brogans, floppy felt hat, and tattered old coat with a bottle of Mad Dog 20/20 wrapped in a paper sack smelling like an old wino.

Willie then asked Jeff if he knew where an old junkyard was. Jeff replied, "What do you need a junkyard for?"

Willie said, “Let’s go. I will show you when we get there.” They pulled into an old junkyard where Jeff knew the owner. They got out and approached the shop. Willie asked, “Do you know this guy?”

Jeff said, “I know him very well.”

Willie replied, “See if he will loan us an old junker that barely runs.” The man agreed to let them use an old clunker but told them it didn’t have a tag. With this, Willie laughed and rolled his head and said, “I’ve got plenty of tags in my trunk.” Jeff looked at him with a concerned stare for a few seconds and decided to go with Willie’s plan. He knew this was going to be a whole lot of fun, and besides, watching Willie was learning experience!

The two drove around the local citrus migrant camps without any luck at the first two. When they got to the labor camp at Twin Lakes, they struck pay dirt. They saw a couple of men standing around a smudge pot to get warm and saw a brand-new white Chevrolet sitting by the old beat-up cars and trucks. Bingo!

With this, Willie said, “Just sit in the car and watch and learn.” The wino went to work. He staggered up to the smudge pot, with the Mad Dog in the paper sack, where all the pickers were talking. Willie said, “Do you know where I can find a job?”

Some fellas spoke up and said, “We’re not hiring today.”

Willie took a swig of that Mad Dog 20/20 and asked if anybody wanted a swig. Then the drunk wino came out. Willie yelled at the top of his voice, “Call the law! Call the law.”

The boss spoke up. “What are you talking about?”

He said, “I forgot to tell you I scraped the side of that new Chevrolet when I pulled in. Call the law. Call the law now.” He was staggering around the smudge pot; all the migrants had a dismayed look on their faces.

One spoke up and said, “Let’s go look at my car.”

Willie asked, “Is that your new car?”

The fruit picker replied, “Yes, it is. It’s just a small scrape. Don’t worry about it.”

Willie kept staggering around with the Mad Dog in his hand, yelling, “Call the law! Call the law! We have to report this.”

The migrant worker said, “No, it’s my car, and it’s okay.”

It was all Jeff could do to keep from rolling out of the car and laughing but knew he had to do his part. So he sat and watched the rest of the show. What happened next was unbelievable. Willie asked, "How do I know this is your car?"

The migrant worker replied, "I have the keys in my pocket."

Willie took another swig of Mad Dog and said, "Let me see the keys."

Jeff began to figure out what was coming next. He had to put the man in the car and control of the vehicle to make a good auto theft case. At this time, Willie the Wino asked the man to prove that it was his car. The man got into the new Chevrolet and started the engine with the key that had the tag on it from the dealership.

In an instant, Willie the Wino began his transformation and waved for Jeff to come over to the car. Willie then took his old floppy hat, stuck it in his back overalls pocket, pulled out his ID and badge, leaned over in the car, and with a big smile said, "I am Deputy Willie Post from the Hernando County Sheriff's Office, and you are under arrest for auto theft." All the thief could do was stutter and muddier as Jeff and Willie cuffed him and walked him back to the old jalopy that they had driven to the labor camp.

As they pulled out of the migrant camp, the car thief was heard to mumble, "I'll be damned. I've been arrested a lot of times, a lot of places, for a lot of things. But I've never been arrested by a damned wino and taken to jail in a junk car."

Over the years, Willie and Jeff became close friends. Willie was always trying to get Jeff to go to old Mexico with him to his wife's village. Jeff was afraid he might like it too much.

Jeff Duval realized that Willie Post was crazy like a fox. From that day on, Jeff knew he was working with a unique professional.

Jeff and Willie were riding around one night, and Willie said, "Let's take a supper break. We will go to my house." They went by the office and he called his wife at home. She only spoke Spanish, and he started rattling off to her. When she answered the phone, Willie started off by saying, "*Yokedo abla me amore.* Hello." With that, they were off to Willie's to eat supper. When they arrived at the gate, they were met by a big German shepherd. Willie said, "Don't get out. He only understands Mexican." And with the looks of the teeth of that big German shepherd, Jeff knew he didn't have love on his mind.

They then drove on to the house. It was a little white frame house and very old. As they walked in the back door, his wife was standing at the stove making some of the best taco's Jeff had ever eaten. As he looked around the room, he saw what appeared to be a girl sitting on a couch facing the other way. She had long beautiful shiny black hair. After introducing Jeff to his wife in Spanish, he walked over to the couch and told the girl to stand up and turn around. He spoke to her, and she turned around and started walking toward Jeff. She was a very beautiful señorita. She extended her hand, and Willie spoke to her again, and she shook hands with Jeff and bowed her head and smiled.

Willie asked, "What do you think, Jeff?"

Jeff said, "I think she is a beautiful young woman."

At which time, everyone sat down at the table. Willie was the only one who understood English. His two sons had already been put to bed, Cypress Post and Cedar Post. As they sat eating a delicious Mexican meal, Willie said, "How would you like to have her for your wife?"

Jeff asked, "That would be wonderful, but I'm already married, and besides, how would I communicate with her?"

Willie said, "Y'all could figure that out. Think about it. She's a beautiful young girl, right?"

Jeff replied, "Well, yes, that is true."

He said, "Once you got her, there are some things you do not want to do."

Jeff asked, "What is that, Willie?"

"Never teach her anymore English than what you want her to know. Never teach her how to drive. Never give her a credit card or tell her anything about a charge account. You will have a good wife for the rest of your life and will not have anything to worry about. She came from a village in old Mexico and lived in an adobe hut with dirt floors. You can rent a little house like I got and use orange crates for chairs and a wire spool for a kitchen table. She would think she is living in the White House."

Jeff replied, "Willie, I am appreciative of the offer and I appreciate you introducing me to the young lady. She seemed to be a very nice person."

After eating, they left and went back to work. Jeff later told Bobbie about the experience at Willie's house. Bobbie looked at Jeff and said, "Oh really!" There was never any further conversation about it again.

Jeff had always heard stories about Willie's years before they had met. He had heard that Willie would set the alarm in his house before he went to old Mexico. So, one evening while on patrol, Jeff asked him if the stories about the briefcase were true. Willie said, "Well, I'm going to Mexico in about two weeks, and I will take you to the house before I leave and show you my burglar alarm," and they left it at that. Sure enough, the evening before he left, they rode out to the little white house. They went into the back door. Willie took Jeff to the bedroom, and on the bed, there was a leather briefcase.

Willie said, "I would let you open it, but you are a friend. Take your flashlight, and I'm going to let you peer in it with your flashlight. Don't get to close. Take your flashlight and peer in the crack."

He did as Willie had instructed. He had his flashlight on when Willie cracked open the briefcase, barely open, so he could see what slick tricks the fox had in store. About a half second after Willie had cracked open the briefcase, there was a loud thud on the top of the briefcase. Jeff jumped back and yelled, "That's a damn big rattlesnake. Are you crazy?"

Willie just rolled his head back and laughed and said, "What do you think the bad guy is going to do? I would probably jump out a window and get the hell out of here, and I sure wouldn't come knowing that big boy was in the house."

He asked Willie, "How do you catch him when you get home?"

Willie answered, "I learned how to catch them years ago in old Mexico. It's not hard to do if you know what you are doing."

With this, the two amigos hit the dusty trail and went back to work. Jeff knew now that the stories he had heard for many years were true and thought to himself, *That would be a very good deterrent. Anybody with a half of a brain and one eye ain't coming back to a house full of rattlesnakes.*

After a few years, the migrant camps closed in Hernando County because of the freezing winters. Willie decided to go farther south, somewhere down around Glade County or Lake Okeechobee, where the migrant workers were and that is where he fit in best. Jeff really hated to see his friend leave. They had become close friends over the years.

Willie would occasionally call Jeff over the years to see how he was doing and to just talk. They would always talk about all the good times they had and how many bad guys they had put away.

Near the end of their talk, Willie said, "I want to tell you something, Jeff."

He asked, "What is that, Willie?"

"I've always thought a lot of you, and you have been a very good law enforcement officer and a very good friend to me." Jeff felt a little strange. He had never shown any emotions, never!

Seven months later, in November, Jeff got to thinking about his old friend Willie and the words he said to him. Jeff called his cell phone number and his wife answered.

He said, "Ms. Post, this is Willie's old friend, Jeff Duval."

She said, "Willie dead."

Jeff was standing in the yard looking at the blue sky and clouds. Her words took his breath. *This cannot be.* When he was able to speak again, he asked, "What did you say?"

She answered, "Willie dead. Willie dead." The words were true, but Jeff could not believe this was happening. He told her how much he loved ole Willie.

Then she said, "You talk to Cypress?"

He replied, "Yes, ma'am."

When he talked to Cypress Post, he said, "I want to tell you some things about your dad. He was one of the best friends that I had in law enforcement. He was a unique person. He was wise beyond words, and that is what helped make him a legend in Florida law enforcement. I will really miss him. I enjoyed our talks and was looking forward to coming down to south Florida to visit. I truly believe your dad is in a lot better place than we are. I think he earned his way to the pearly gates."

Jeff does not know where Cypress Post or Cedar Post is today. He said he did know one thing for sure—if they were half the man their daddy was, they are good men!

This story is dedicated to all the law enforcement officers in the State of Florida who knew Willie Post, a Florida law enforcement legend!

GOPHER SOLVED THE KIDNAPPING

In the spring of 1980, a deputy was dispatched to the east side of the county, a very rural area known as Ridge Manor Estates, north of Highway 50 on 301. It was a very desolate area that had been developed, but at that time, it had no homes, just gravel roads for miles crisscrossing the sand hills.

Once, a body of a female who had been murdered in Pinellas County was brought to Ridge Manor Estates and dumped in the sand hills. The body had been there a few months, and most of the evidence was destroyed because of the elements. Law enforcement had to use her dental records and the jewelry she was wearing to identify who she was. The investigators on the case were able to track down a person of interest but had no way of tying him to the murder. This one walked. There have been other bodies dumped in the area over the years.

One afternoon, a young deputy was on routine patrol and decided to ride out in the desolate area to see what he could find. You never know, you could find another body.

After riding around several roads, he came to a cul-de-sac and saw a light blue Ford sitting off the lime rock road. He chose not to approach the car to play it safe. After waiting for approximately forty-five minutes, no one came back to the car. He figured it was time to ease his way up to the car and check it out. He walked very slowly, just in case he might be jumped by a bad guy coming back from dumping a car. You could not be too careful, he thought. He wrote the tag number in his hand just in case. As he got near the car, he stopped and listened. He heard noises coming from the trunk of the car. *Dang, there is somebody in the trunk of that car, I knew it! This will probably be a big case.* As he eased even closer, he could hear the body trying to scratch or claw loose from whatever he was tied to, the young deputy thought. Now it was time to be even more cautious. Who knew what was lurking behind that tree over there with the nearest backup nearly thirty miles away? The deputy went ahead and asked the dispatcher to have someone head his way, thinking all the time they would never find him because the other deputies didn't know much about this area.

The young deputy could see the sun was setting low in the sky. He decided to move even closer to the car. He knew an old trick some old fella had taught him a long time ago. Pick up a stick and put it to the body of the car and put the other end to your ear, and it will convey sound so you can hear what is going on inside better.

Now, in those days, we didn't have the bionic ear they have today. So you had to think outside the box, somewhat like MacGyver, but the stick did not help a whole lot, just made the noise louder. It sounded like someone crawling around in the trunk. He figured they must have their mouth duct-taped. It was getting late, and dusk was beginning to set in. He knew he had to do something quick. He got a crowbar out of his trunk, and he was just about to pop that trunk open when a little old black man came lurking out the woods with a croker sack with a long piece of wire and said, "Hey, mister. What are you doing?"

The deputy looked over to see a little old man. He looked like he was in his eighties. The deputy was a little startled and said, "I'll be asking the questions. What in the world are you doing out here in this wilderness with a croker sack and a piece of wire?"

The old man answered, "Man, I'm catching gophers."

The deputy asked, "Catching gophers? What you got in the trunk of this car? Open it up if you would, sir."

He said, "I sure will." The old man popped the trunk. There must have been fifteen gopher turtles running around in that trunk.

The young deputy was so disappointed that a gopher had solved this case. He thought surely, he had a major kidnapping or maybe even more, and it turned out to be an eighty-year-old man huntin' gophers. At this time, the young deputy called dispatch with a somewhat disappointed voice and said, "You can 10-22 the backup [which meant cancel]. A gopher has solved this case. I'm 10-8 [which meant back on the road again]."

WILD AND WOOLY NIGHTS

. . . .

My name is Skip Gossett. I lived in Hillsborough County for many years until I decided to move to Brooksville in Hernando County in the early 1980s.

I had become good friends with Sheriff Melvin Kelly and would be around the office when the deputies would come in. One morning when I was visiting Sheriff Kelly, he introduced me to Sgt. Jeff Duval. After getting to know Jeff, he became a family friend. He asked me one day if I would like to do a ride along, which I accepted. After that night, we became good friends. It seems we had a lot of things in common. I soon joined the Sheriff's Posse and became more involved with my friends at the sheriff's office.

I knew from riding with the deputies at night they were getting a lot of calls on Friday and Saturday nights east of town at the Tiki Hut Lounge, which was adjacent to the local bowling alley and lounge. It seemed as though a bunch of roughens were gathering on Friday and Saturday nights in both parking lots, throwing beer bottles back and forth and busting them in the parking lot. Jerry, the owner of the Tiki Hut, would call in on Friday and Saturday nights around ten thirty, asking to have the troublemakers removed from the parking lot, and so would the owner of the bowling alley and lounge. Since there were only three deputies on in the county at night, the sergeant would float and take calls and would usually take the ones around town. Most of the roughens knew Jeff personally because they had grown up together.

One Saturday night, Jeff and I pulled into the Tiki Hut parking lot, and we noticed an older gentleman in the crowd, who we recognized as Jimmy Lane, a local power company worker and somewhat of a smart ass. He stopped his car a few feet from the crowd because he figured they were drunk, and he didn't know what to expect. As we stood behind the door of the patrol car and Jeff started his routine spiel about leaving the parking lot and cleaning up the bottles, Jimmy Lane spoke up and now seemed to be the ringleader of the crowd. He seemed to be a little drunk as he said, "Why the hell don't you get out of here and leave these young men alone?"

At which time, Jeff replied, "Maybe you are unaware of the trouble they have been causing these two businesses."

Some of the members of the crowd started echoing Jimmy's thoughts. About this time, Jeff could feel his temperature rise, as Jimmy the new spokesman said, "Why don't you get back in that car and go back to town."

Jeff replied, "When they start picking up these bottles and throwing them in the trash, we just might do that. I'm here on a lawful call, doing my job, and the best thing you can do is stand back and be quiet."

We could feel Jimmy Lane stare as he was trying to impress the young men. Jeff had never had a run-in with Jimmy before. They started picking up the bottles and cleaning up the mess, and we drove over to the bowling alley and told the owner they were cleaning up the area and would be leaving.

We knew the other deputies on duty that night heard the radio conversation with dispatch in Brooksville. Rick Singer said, "Sarge, you need any help?"

The sergeant advised, "10-54, everything seems to be clearing out."

There were approximately eighteen to twenty people in the crowd, and they were slowly leaving. We then drove back to the sheriff's office in Brooksville, and we had a good cup of jailhouse coffee to decompress.

As we walked through the door, the chief dispatcher, Ronnie Elliott, was smiling and said, "They are getting to be a real problem."

Jeff replied, "Yep, they are beginning to get under my skin, Ronnie."

As we came back into the front office, a friend of Jeff's and fellow deputy, Big Wayne Pennerger, was coming through the door smiling. He went in and got a cup of coffee and came back out to the counter and said, "Hey, Sarge, how long has this been going on? About three months?"

Jeff replied, "Yes, on and off. The businesspeople are tired of it and have called the sheriff and he has advised me to put a stop to this mayhem. He told me if I had to lock some local people up, do what you must do. We can't have these people harassing local businesspeople. Wayne, if you have any more trouble and I'm not here, put some butts in jail. That's the only way they are going to learn. You try to be good and some people just will not comply. So now we know what we're going to do."

Next Saturday night, Jeff got a call from dispatch saying there was some kind of ruckus in the parking lot at the Tiki Hut and someone was brandishing a rifle around the parking lot. The dispatch also said, "Jerry the bar owner thinks some of the boys are too young to be drinking and Jimmy Lane is buying the beer for them." I had kind of figured that from last weekend's encounter. At this point in time, Brooksville advised, "10-18 to the Tiki Hut Lounge," which means lights and sirens and hurry up.

As we slid into the parking lot facing the crowd, I noticed Jimmy Lane holding a .30-30 down to his side. As we stepped out of the patrol car, Jeff unsnapped his holster and stood behind the door. Jeff asked Jimmy Lane to put the gun back in his truck. He seemed ready for a fight. The one thing you learned early on is you never back up. If you do, you are a marked man and will never make it in law enforcement. At which time, Jeff told Lane, "I'm not requesting. I'm giving you a lawful order to put that rifle back in the truck."

He replied, "Screw you, Mr. Deputy," and raised the gun in Jeff's direction.

Jeff was standing behind the patrol car door, out in the open. "18 to 11, I'm 10-51, 10-18. ETA three minutes." We heard Ricky John, from FHP, advise he would be there shortly. As Jeff was trying to calm the situation, the other men were cheering Lane on, as we stood frozen behind the door, and Jeff never had time to unholster his weapon.

Ricky John slide into the parking lot sideways with Pennerger right beside him. They had their twelve-gauge shotguns drawn as they jumped out of their patrol cars, with the dust flying, and said, "Drop the weapon or you are a dead man, and don't anyone else move."

We sure felt a sigh of relief when we heard them charging in. We knew they had our backs covered. Jeff then unholstered his .41 Magnum and pointed it toward Jimmy Lane and said, "Jimmy, it's your decision. Drop that gun on the parking lot. You threatened three officers." He then cocked the Smith & Wesson Magnum and told him once more to drop the weapon. At which time, he did, and Jeff slowly uncocked his weapon and holstered it, and all three officers moved forward. Jeff put eight people in the back of his patrol car. RJ and Big Wayne Pennerger started loading their cars.

We noticed three men had not said anything all night. They had lived down the road from Jeff since they were kids and were pretty good young men. Jeff said, "I'm going to give you guys a break since y'all didn't say too much tonight. If you come down to the county jail when we're booking these hombres and cause a ruckus, I'm going to arrest all three of you. Now, go home."

After getting them all down to the county jail on Jefferson Street and started the booking process, the three brothers showed up cursing and wanting to know what their friends were charged with and causing a ruckus. Jeff walked out on the ole colonial porch and said, "Men, come on in. You are under arrest. I'm a man of my word." With this, the parties in the parking lot stopped.

Jeff thanked RJ and Wayne Pennerger for having their back that night. It will never be forgotten.

DARK DAYS

I recall a story Sgt. Jeff Duval relayed to me about a brawl that occurred at the Gold Dollar Bar and Saloon about a gang of ruffians known throughout the county. Drinking and fighting were common to them. He said he was dispatched to the scene, and when he walked in, he walked up to the bar and spoke to the bartender and asked what the problem was. The bartender said, "That group of Logans and their friends. I want them out of my bar. They've been causing trouble all night."

As Jeff turned to his left and looked at the group, he recognized them immediately. He had known them since they were children and shared a neighborhood at one point in time. Jeff said he knew the family back to their grandma, whom he called Grandma Logan, a sweet old lady with a kind heart. However, the younger group of this family were prone to drink and fight. He thought they might listen to reason since they knew him, and he had not had much trouble with them before, but there was a new face in the crowd that was not familiar that was dating one of the girls.

As he approached the table, he spoke to one of the girls in the family that he knew very well, Billie Sue, a tall lanky blonde that had somewhat of a reputation of being a hardnose. Jeff told her what the bartender said, that they had been causing trouble and he wanted them removed from the bar. Billie Sue said, "We ain't causing any trouble. Just having fun." He told her it was not his decision to make. He was just doing his job, and they had to leave or be charged with trespassing. Jeff walked out to the car and radioed for backup. He knew there was going to be trouble. He couldn't handle this group and whoever else might jump in with this bunch because they were known to be bad. Deputy John Whitman answered the call, and he was en route, but it would take him a little bit to get there.

When Whitman got there, they walked back into the Gold Dollar, went straight to the table where the Logans were seated, and said, "Billie Sue, y'all gotta go."

One of the Logan brothers stood up and said, "We're going no friggin' where."

At which time, Jeff replied, "You're leaving this bar now." Jeff walked around Billie Sue and took Harry Logan by the arm. At that point, he jerked away, and the melee was on, Jeff, John, and about ten other people in the bar. Harry Logan ran to a screen door, and Jeff gave pursuit and told him he was under arrest. Jeff ran through the screen door after Harry. He was determined to catch Harry, but the young man was too fast. After about a forty-yard sprint, he knew he wasn't going to catch him, so he slung is Kel-Light, missing the subject with great disappointment. Harry ran into the dark leaving Jeff to find his Kel-Light since it had gone out. Jeff scrambled around in the grass trying to find it, and he finally felt it.

Jeff jumped up and ran toward the bar remembering that John Whitman was there by himself. As he ran around the corner in the parking lot, he saw a pile of bodies. He hollered for John, "Where are you, Whitman?" And he heard, "Help me, Jeff! They've got my damn gun. I can't find my gun." At this time, Jeff unholstered his .44 Smith & Wesson Magnum and fired a round into the ground. That .44 Magnum sounded like a cannon as it echoed around the building.

"I'm not going to let y'all kill him. I want the damn gun, now." He was heard to yell, "You dirtbags better get off him." They began to jump up off John, and Jeff stood there with his Magnum pointed to the ground. "I'm not going to holster this gun until I know where John's gun is. Stand up and stand still. I don't want to shoot anyone, but I want that damn gun, and I want it now."

Jeff opened his car door and called, "11 Brooksville, 10-24, 10-24. Send help immediately."

He then heard John say, "They dropped the gun. I heard it hit the ground."

In the dim light of the parking lot, it was hard to see who had the gun, but John grabbed it as soon as it hit the ground. They could hear sirens coming from both directions from far off. The Logans and their buddies were still running their mouths, cussing the deputies and wanting to be rowdy. Jeff stood his ground with the .44 Smith & Wesson Magnum in his hand and told them to move forward and stand in a group as Whitman circled behind them so no one would escape. The city police were pulling in the driveway, and a state trooper was pulling in the parking lot behind him. Jeff said that he was feeling some relief as they wheeled into the parking lot with their lights and sirens. He was afraid there was going to be a shootin' before they got backup.

The roundup began with the trooper, the two city police, John Whitman, and Sgt. Jeff Duval handcuffing them and placing them in patrol cars. Jeff and John were the only two injuries in the melee. Two against twelve is not very good odds.

As Jeff looked over toward John Whitman's patrol car, he saw a posse member, Leo May, leaning against John Whitman's patrol car. He said to the posse member, "Hey, hero, why in hell doesn't your shirt have any blood or dirt on it?"

Leo replied, "I didn't want to get involved."

Jeff looked over at Whitman and told him, "Take this posse member back to the sheriff's office and take his badge and equipment. We don't have any place in our department for a coward."

When they arrived at the sheriff's office and got the subjects booked, they thanked the City of Brooksville Officers Ron Batten and George Arthur and the FHP for their assistance. The sheriff came out and said, "Good job, men. Now you two go to the hospital and get checked out. You're all bloody and beat up. Then you can go home." John Whitman and Jeff discussed the story as they drove to the hospital. They were there for a couple of hours and released. John Whitman and Jeff had been friends since the sixth grade and remained good friends until John passed over.

Jeff said that he had no way of foreseeing the dark days that lay ahead from a routine brawl at the Gold Dollar Bar and Saloon.

Working the night shift a few weeks later, Sergeant Duval came in from the east side of the county to fuel his patrol car. When he went inside to sign the ticket, the dispatcher said, "They're having some trouble in the back of the jail with one of the Logan boys."

He replied, "Well, I've got to get back to the east side. There is something I'm working on. Call me if you need assistance." He was the only supervisor on that night.

Jeff hadn't gotten a mile down the road before the dispatcher called and said, "10-19, return to the office." He turned around and went back and walked in and asked what was going on. One of the night jailers in charge came out to speak to him and said, "That Junior Logan had beat up another inmate and was threatening others in the bullpen and refused to go back in his bunk cell."

At this point, Jeff asked the night jailer in charge, "What do you want to do? I've known Junior since he was a baby. Maybe he will listen to me."

As the two jailers and Jeff walked into the area, he saw Junior standing at the table. Junior had grown into a tall muscular young man, standing approximately six feet, three inches. He was standing in the bullpen alone as the others had been put in their bunk cells. Junior was refusing to go after a fight with another inmate.

Jeff said, "Junior, what's the problem?"

Junior's replied, "There was no damn problem until you came along."

Jeff said, "I've known you since you were a baby, and your grandmother was like my own grandmother. Now, Junior, you're in enough trouble. You beat up another inmate and threatened others. Why don't you just comply and go into your bunk like they've asked you to do." He was then told by the jailer that he would be placed in a single cell if it became necessary.

At this time, the cell block was open. Jeff said, "Let me walk in first. Maybe I can reason with him." The two jailers walked in behind Jeff. He knew that he was trained not to go into a cell block, but he didn't feel like he was in danger from the other inmates. All he had to worry about was Junior Logan.

As he moved slowly toward Logan, he kept trying to low key the situation, said, "Junior, come on, man, just back into your cell. Everything will be fine. You don't need any more trouble."

Logan moved back toward the cell door putting his arms out. He began to act irrational and said, "I'm not going in there."

Jeff made direct eye contact with Junior and asked him again to go into his cell. Before Jeff knew it, he was struck like lighting with a karate kick directly to his testicles. He dropped to the floor like a sack of potatoes. He felt his body shaking as his eyes rolled back in his head. Being kicked that hard, it felt like his groin was swelling to the size of a softball. He recalled it being the worst pain he ever felt in his life. For a while all, he recalled was balling up in a fetal position unable to move and sweating profusely. When he was able to realize what was going on, he turned his head, not able to straighten his legs. He could hear a commotion of a rumble going on in the cell block. Struggling to see what was going on through the pain, he saw the two jailers and Deputy Dan Mancini trying to gain control of a madman. He was biting and kicking at the officers.

Jeff said he then crawled in a ball over to where Junior was and was able to reach around to his back pocket and remove a slap jack and swung it in the direction of Junior's head. The first swing hit his shoulder, and the next swing hit him somewhere on the top of his head. At this point, they dragged Junior out toward a single cell screaming, hollering, kicking, biting, and yelling, "You sons of bitches ain't taking me in there."

At this point, Jeff was still in a tight fetal position on the floor, sweating profusely and in pain and still unable to move. You could not humanly imagine. He said he remembered Robert Slimborn running back and telling him they were calling an ambulance to take him to the hospital. He said he told them to just help him up as he could not walk on his own. One of the jailers and one of the deputies, one on each side, dragged Jeff through the lobby and helped him sit in a chair. Jeff told the dispatcher to cancel the ambulance and that his wife was a nurse at the hospital and he was not going to the hospital and he refused to go into an ambulance, like he had done many times before when injured. He said he had a phobia about ambulances because he had loaded so many bodies and body parts in the back of ambulances and always refused to go if he was conscious.

The jailer and the deputy helped Jeff to his patrol car as he drove out the driveway thinking that there was nothing at the hospital that could help him with this injury. He thought one of his tentacles was busted. He knew his wife could help him with his problem by packing ice on his injury better than a nurse or doctor at the hospital.

Three weeks later, he was able to stand up right finally. He sustained a very serious injury to his tentacles with lots of scar tissue that was discovered later when Dr. Hamoui opened him up to do a vasectomy. Jeff did not return to work for about a week because he could not stand the pain of walking and could not stand straight up due to the injury he sustained.

About two weeks later, the local mullet rapper *the Brooksville Sun* came out with a wild story that an inmate had been handcuffed to the bars in the jail and beaten severely. As soon as Jeff read the story, he went straight to the sheriff's office to meet with the sheriff to see if he had seen the story in the paper. He had not. Jeff said he was outraged and very hurt of such a story that was totally unfounded being printed without anyone asking a question to him or the sheriff's office and any of the other employees that were on duty the night of the incident. It was printed as being factual, not alleged anything. This was very hurtful to Jeff and the sheriff. Both were honorable men with pride and dignity and served with honor. Some people just want to believe the worse and take the news media as a matter-of-fact without any forethought or afterthought.

The hellish nightmare had just begun. Some of the people Jeff had arrested over the years were calling the radio station and talking to the newspaper. They wanted to see him hanged. Some of these folks he had known all his life, unfortunately. When you live in a rural county, you have to arrest some of the people you knew growing up!

The hurt ran very deep. The hurt ran a lot deeper than the anger, but both were almost unbearable to him and the sheriff. He had worked so hard in the community and had such a great reputation of helping people that were down and out, like the two young children that he started fund drives for with his own money. He had such a love for working with the people and was well known for this in his community.

After a bell has been rung, it's hard to unring the bell; the lies had been told. Some people wanted Jeff and the other deputies fired or put on administrative leave. An internal investigation was ordered by the sheriff. Jeff was cleared of any wrongdoing a few weeks later. Sheriff Melvin Kelly stood by him and refused to fire or put him on administrative leave because he believed what Jeff had told him. He had faith in the young sergeant. The sheriff once said in a large crowd that he was one of the best deputy sheriffs he had ever seen and was one of the youngest deputies to receive the deputy of the year award in the 1970s.

He continued to work his assigned duties for the next two years withstanding stress and heartbreak and struggled each day and night to do what had to be done to perform his duties under such intense pressure.

Sheriff Melvin Kelly had known Jeff since the age of five. Jeff remembered one time when he was about ten years old, he was playing baseball with some other boys in a field in his neighborhood. They didn't have a baseball, so they were using rocks. Jeff threw a rock, breaking a neighbor's window. All the boys scattered running home. That evening, Deputy Melvin Kelly was sent out to investigate the broken window. When the ten-year-old saw the deputy pull in the driveway of his family home, he was very scared. He knew it meant trouble. At this time, Deputy Kelly was invited into the family home by Jeff's mother, Jacqueline Nadine, commonly known as Jackie by most of the town's people. Kelly asked if he could talk to the youngster about a broken window. She said, "Sure, Melvin. Come on into the table and have a seat." As the three sat at the table, Jeff began to sweat and tremble, because he had never been in trouble with the law. His mother asked him if he knew anything about the broken window. At which time, he just shrugged his shoulders. Melvin Kelly looked at Jeff straight in the eye and said, "Son, you have nothing to fear by telling the truth." Melvin had a way of communicating. He was a Southern gentleman. Jeff felt at ease and told the deputy that he had thrown the rock in playing the baseball game in the field and broke the window. As Jeff grew up in Hernando County over the years, he knew and had faith in Melvin Kelly. He never forgot what Melvin had told him at ten years old. Never fear the truth!

The night Melvin Kelly took office, he and Jeff had worked together since 1969. Melvin Kelly was a great mentor and taught Jeff many valuable lessons over the years. The night he took office, he once again told all the deputies he was retaining, "Never lie to me. If you do, you will be fired immediately because I can never trust you again!"

Three of the deputies had testified under oath to a special prosecutor during the second investigation of this matter. Deputy Robert Slimborn, Deputy Ron Asbell, and Deputy Mansinni were charged with lying to the special prosecutor under oath and stripped of their blue line certificate and fired for the beating of Junior Logan. Two others left the county since it was just prior to the election. Jeff said it was his opinion that the men had lied all along trying to lay the blame on him and to gain favor with a possible new incoming sheriff. Jeff was cleared of any wrongdoing by the special prosecutor and the governor of the State of Florida, Bob Graham, after two intense investigations and two years of living a hellish, dark nightmare and hurt!

He was working the midnight shift and would usually only get an hour or two of sleep a day because of the stress.

The phone rang one morning about ten o'clock at his home. He woke up and answered the phone. It was Sheriff Melvin Kelly. The sheriff said, "Jeff, its finally over. We have been cleared of any wrongdoing, and the case is finally over and closed."

He replied, "Thank you, Sheriff, and thanks for standing by me through one of the hardest times of my life." As he hung up the phone, the anguish and hurt of two years finally came bursting out. He went and lay on the bed and wept with relief and resolve and said, "Thank you God almighty."

The next night he was off and fell into a restful sleep like he had not had in two years.

A lot of good people in the county also stood by Jeff and by Sheriff Kelly because they believed the truth.

Jeff was told once as a young man the truth shall set you free. He believed that and experienced a feeling of freedom from the hellish nightmare and returned to his duties with a new resolve.

NOT ALWAYS BY THE BOOK

Another story that Jeff shared with me that I just felt compelled to share. It shows the character of the man and officer that he was. He liked to solve crimes and enjoyed putting a bad guy behind bars and sometimes would push the boundaries to the edge to capture a real criminal. This story is one of those times.

It was a few years after he had been appointed patrol sergeant and opened the Ridge Manor Substation to fulfill a campaign promise Sheriff Kelly had made to the people on the east side of the county. Up until this time, Deputy Leonard "Nig" Mills was able to handle the Ridge Manor area, but with the growth of the county being so rapid in the 1980s, Nig was no longer able to handle the expansion of Zone 3, the east side, which now took in many more miles moving westward toward Brooksville, including Spring Lake.

Nig Mills was a hard-core cracker, old-school kind of guy, that had been hired by Sheriff Sim L. Lowman, as Range Rider back in the 1950s. He was grandfathered into law enforcement. Things began to change in the 1970s. He was the last of the old-timers. He was a real Florida cowboy and was as tough as a keg of railroad spikes.

Jeff had learned a lot from just observing some of the things you couldn't learn at the academy or out of a book on capturing a crook.

Jeff said one evening he was patrolling the rural area of Ridge Manor, and he always made a thorough neighborhood check in the areas from the Withlacoochee River east. One night, he was given a call that there was a suspicious vehicle sitting with its lights out on Idle A While Circle. The nearest backup in those days would be twenty minutes away or longer. You had to handle things sometimes yourself, and that is exactly what Jeff did this particular night. As he approached Idle A While Circle off Ridge Manor Boulevard, he turned the headlights off on the patrol car and proceeded slowly onto Idle A While, holding a flashlight down low out the window to not draw any attention to himself. As he approached the car very slowly, he was able to slip right up behind the bad guy's vehicle sitting in the road in front of a house. At this point in time, he said he called for backup and then proceeded to slip out of his patrol car and slowly walked up just behind the driver, with his hand on the butt of that big Magnum. He tapped on the window, and the subject rolled the window down slowly as Jeff held the flashlight in his eyes so he could not see. He was taken totally by surprise. Jeff asked for his identification, and upon checking, he was found to be wanted out of Pasco County for burglary.

Jeff then said, "Where is your partner? In that house?" The man then became a suspect. Jeff knew that somebody was in the house. This guy was a lookout man, for sure. He then told Jeff his brother was breaking into the house, and he was the lookout man. At this point, Jeff advised him to start his car with the lights off and slip down the road and drive to the sheriff's substation at Highway 301 and Highway 50. The suspect did exactly as he was ordered. Once at the substation, he was given his Miranda warning. After a short interview, the suspect agreed to sign a waiver. It was at that time he admitted he and his brother were there to burglarize the house and other houses in the area and that his brother was still in the house.

Jeff asked him if he would be willing to volunteer to drive back to the scene in his own car. The subject agreed. Jeff advised him he was going with him. The suspect said, "That is fine. I'm not going down by myself." Jeff got into the back seat of the suspect's car, which was dirty and stank, but Jeff would go to almost any length to get the bad guy!

As they proceeded back toward the scene, Jeff was lying on the floorboard with the suspect driving alone in the cold of the night. Jeff could feel the roaches crawling all over him. Had it been rattlesnakes, it would not have made any difference to him. He was bound and determined to get these burglars off the street and into jail.

He told the suspect driving the car, "Don't be stupid and tip your brother off. It will just make it harder on you."

As they slowed to a stop, Jeff got in position behind the passenger seat. The bad guy said, "Here comes my brother. He's probably been looking for me."

Jeff said, "Be really cool."

The other bad guy jumped into the car and slammed the door and said, "Where the hell have you been?"

He said, "I had to drive around a little bit."

As they drove into the night back toward Highway 50, the driver turned left and headed toward the substation and Highway 301. The bad guy in the passenger seat said, "Let's go, brother." He was in a hurry to get back to the French Quarter, commonly known as Lachoochee across the Pasco County line.

The driver did a good job as he was instructed. Now it was time for Jeff to do his job. As they approached Highway 301 and Highway 50 near the substation, Jeff sat up behind the bad guy on the passenger side and laid that cold nickel-plated Magnum alongside the burglar's ear and said, "Brotherman, I'm Sgt. Jeff Duval, Hernando County Sheriff's Office, and y'all are under arrest for burglary. Don't be foolish and do something real stupid at this point."

The burglar then said, "Mister, there isn't enough money in the bank to make me do something stupid right now."

They pulled into the substation. Jeff was holding his pistol at his side following the two suspects. The backup unit arrived as they walked up to the front door. It was ole Billy Donn, who got out of his patrol car, and said, "Damn, John Wayne, I see you already have things under control."

Jeff kind of laughed. "Well, if I had waited on you, they would have gotten away, and that would not have made the sheriff really happy, and I would not have slept very well myself."

The two were booked into the Hernando County Jail, and a warrant was served out of Pasco County. They both spent time in the Florida State Penitentiary, in Raiford, Florida, after it was all said and done.

Back in those days, we just had to do what had to be done. There were not enough deputies to do the job of serving the people of Hernando County. You could not depend on any help being available lots of times. You had to take a risk and do things out of the box or you could die. It's called survival.

AHAB THE WILDMAN

Along about 1982, Sheriff Kelly created the first marine patrol unit in Hernando County. The headlines in the local newspaper read, "Hernando County's First Bear on the Water." The paper even included a picture of the patrol boat. Sergeant Duval was appointed to operate the twenty-one-foot Mako Marine Patrol Boat. It was fully equipped with lights, siren, sheriff's star, and radios to patrol the coastline of the Gulf of Mexico, rivers, and lakes of Hernando County.

Since Jeff had been a fishing buddy of the sheriff's, he knew Jeff could operate the boat, whether it was an airboat or any other type of boat since Jeff was born on the Gulf of Mexico and knew all about the water and water safety.

A lot of his friends and acquaintances were always asking him to take a ride in the county's new patrol boat. The investigator for the state attorney's office, Everett, went out with Jeff one Saturday and found out the job was not always fun. It was hot in an open boat along the coastline. Jeff and Everett had been stopping boaters checking for safety equipment all day. Back in the early days, the deputy on the boat had to wear a full uniform. In later years, things would be more comfortable, but not at that time. Lots of times after being out in the hot uniform, Jeff would ease the big boat up through the narrow shallows of the Weeki Wachee River at the end of the day and take a cool refreshing dive overboard in the river up by the springs.

During that time, a lot of alcohol was being consumed on the river by the tubers. More and more people were coming to enjoy the cool spring water every year. It was getting to the point the tubers were beginning to cause trouble with the homeowners along the rivers and canals by throwing beer cans and trash along the riverbanks. Jeff would have his hands full when things would begin to get out of hand when the tubers would have too much alcohol. The County finally passed an ordinance banning alcohol on the Weeki Wachee River. The county still had problems with people bringing in alcohol. Arrests were being made, and alcohol was being confiscated.

He told me that he saw a local drug runner that he knew moving up and down the river regularly. One Saturday, he stopped the young fella for speeding in a "No Wake Zone." Upon stopping the boat, he saw a bag of pot and arrested the drug runner, confiscated and impounded the boat and motor, and booked the young man in the county jail.

An old friend of his, who was a local undertaker in Brooksville, asked if he could ride along on the boat with him one Saturday. Jeff told him it was not all fun and games and that sometimes you have to run to stranded people. It's hot and aggravating dealing with people who have been drinking on the water. You may have to take a call out in the gulf or things like that, but the undertaker persisted he wanted to ride along. Jeff told the undertaker to meet him at the Weeki Wachee boat ramp on Saturday at ten o'clock in the morning at Roger's Park near the bridge.

The day started off with a run out into the gulf, after making their way down the river to the dock at Bayport, out in the channel, checking fishermen for safety equipment. About two hours later, they worked their way back to the dock by the bridge for a rest. Upon docking in the small canal, adjacent to the river bridge, they noticed someone walking along the river's edge acting strange.

The fella seemed to be bending over and picking things up and examining them and throwing them, but there wasn't anything there. At that time, Jeff told the undertaker to look at the guy walking down the riverbank acting strange, since he's beginning to annoy people. Jeff said he and the undertaker kept an eye on the stranger because he was moving closer to where they were docked.

They noticed the guy would stop along the tables where people were enjoying their picnic lunch on the beach. The stranger would go from table to table beginning to annoy the whole crowd. There were approximately two hundred people at Roger's Park that day. About fifty of them were high school students that Jeff knew. Jeff said, "Mr. Undertaker, he's coming over our way."

When he got down to the dock where Jeff and David were sitting, he said, "I found a wallet." Jeff noticed he had a foreign accent. The man continued, "I want to turn it in."

Jeff said, "Thank you. That's great. I will have to put it in an evidence bag and find out who it belongs to. I will need your name as person who found the wallet."

The strange man replied, "I will not give you my name," in broken English.

Jeff knew he was not an American-born citizen by the broken English and simply said, "I must have your name to go on the incident report that I have to file."

The stranger looked at Jeff and replied simply, "No."

The undertaker took notice and said, "You better watch this guy. He doesn't appear to be normal to me."

The strange man walked over to a table of picnickers and sat down between them. Jeff said, "That must be his family," and told the undertaker to watch the boat because he was going to talk to them. When he spoke to the man where the stranger had sat down next to, they were having fried chicken and potato salad and he said to the man, "That sure looks good. Is this your brother or relative that just sat down with you folks?"

The man's reply sent a strange feeling up Jeff's spine. The man said, "We don't know who he is." He then asked the strange man for his name again and explained why he needed his name. Jeff then put his hand on the strange man's shoulder and told him they needed to have a talk over by the boat.

The strange man jumped up and jerked away and picked up a six-foot fence post that had come off the fence near the boat dock and began to swing at Jeff. The undertaker yelled, "What do you want me to do?"

Jeff said, "Take care of the boat." Jeff told him to take the mic and say, "Marine 1 to Brooksville, 10-24, 10-24 [send help immediately] at the boat ramp, Weeki Wachee Bridge." At this point in time, Jeff was trying to take him physically. He did not want to use deadly force. About that time, the guy dropped the fence post and ran to the top of the bridge with Jeff right behind him. He was thinking, *Oh my, he's going to jump into the river*, but instead the man ran over and under the superstructure of the Weeki Wachee Bridge and began to crawl like a spider under the bridge. Jeff noticed an elderly couple in a johnboat fishing under the bridge. The elderly lady said, "He's messing up my fishing. Take this paddle and knock him down." Suddenly, Jeff saw something large and shiny in the guy's hand. It looked like a bowie knife, a shiny very large knife. At this point, things began to happen very rapidly. Jeff was then in fear for his life but was trying to hang onto the structure and trying to back away from the man swinging this knife. Jeff yelled at the undertaker, "Bring the boat now. Get the boat under him." He was thinking that if he had to shoot the guy, he will fall directly on the undertaker.

There were several young fellas on the riverbank he recognized from town chanting, "Get him, Jeff. Get him. Get him, Jeff. Get him."

It was the first time he had seen a bewildered look on the undertaker's face. Now he was thinking, *I've got to make a split-second decision*. Things were going down quick. David kept maneuvering the boat under the bridge. The elderly lady in the johnboat anchored under the bridge and said, "Here, son," handing Jeff a paddle. "See if you can knock that big knife out of his hand." Things were happening so fast, but Jeff could hear the scream of a patrol car coming his way.

Jim slid across the bridge smoking his tires and said, "I'm here." Jeff heard a second patrol car on the east side of the bridge. He heard Lanney say, "Don't shoot him. Don't shoot him. We're here." About that time, the madman took a swipe with that big knife, and Jeff said, "Don't shoot him. Hell, come down here and let him swing a bowie knife at you a few times. I should have already taken him out." About that time, the madman swung the knife wildly striking the paddle and sticking it firmly in place. Jeff said he then jerked the paddle downward, jerking the paddle out of the guy's hand. The guy lost his balance and fell into the river, alongside the boat, with the undertaker looking in awe.

The boys on the riverbank, ole tall George, Scooter, and several other high school boys, jumped in and grabbed the madman like a big gator and said, "Where do you want him, Jeff?"

Jeff replied, "Bring him over here to the boat. The undertaker can have him." As the undertaker pulled him over into the boat with a big moan, he then looked at Jeff with an odd look and said, "I don't think I'll ride along with you anymore."

Jeff climbed on the bow of the boat and told his friend, "Let's go back to the dock," where they were met by Lanney and Jimmy and a large crowd of onlookers. Jeff thanked the young men that came to his aid and said, "I will never forget you guys helping us today."

The local mullet wrapper, the *Brooksville Sun*, came out in a couple of days and did a half-page story on "Deputy Jousted with a Wildman, Shifiee Ja, Under the Weeki Wachee Bridge."

"Deputy Duval was able to knock the large Bowie Knife out of the Wildman's hand with a paddle that an elderly lady gave him to help take out a possible killer."

It was later discovered the madman was wanted by Pasco County on a warrant and by the FBI and had been deported back to the Sand Dunes.

THE OLD MAN AND HIS DOG

• • • • • • • • • • • • •

Jeff relayed a story about an old man and his dog to me. One morning around eight o'clock, he was coming out of Alice's Restaurant after having breakfast. He remembered thinking he was glad he didn't get a call during breakfast, like so many other times.

As he looked out toward Highway 41, he noticed an old man, in a tattered old jacket, pulling a little red wagon with a bedroll and a little scroungy dog in the wagon behind him. He said his curiosity always told him there is a story behind every traveler. The old man looked weathered and unshaven as he trudged along pulling his little red wagon.

Jeff said he then walked down to the edge of the road to meet the old man and to find out what his story was. After he introduced himself, he asked the old gentleman where he was headed. To the best of his recollection, the old man said he was going somewhere down around Lakeland. He further said it had taken him all night to walk to Brooksville from Tampa. The old man seemed to be earnest in his demeanor and seemed like a likeable old fella. Jeff told me once before he never failed meeting someone like this and put himself in their shoes and hoped that if the day ever came that someone would reach out to him with a helping hand.

About this time, the old weathered gray gentleman said, "Sir, I won't ask for myself, but I was wondering if you could buy my dog a hamburger. I know he is very hungry."

"Yes, sir, I will. Follow me up the parking lot to the door and wait there." He then walked inside and told Pinky, the waitress, to fix up three hamburger sacks and a large coffee to go. He then walked back outside and gave two of the hamburger sacks to the old man and asked him if he minded if he fed the last hamburger to the little dog.

Jeff then asked, "What's the dog's name?"

The old man replied, "I just call him Pooch."

As Jeff began to unwrap the fresh beef, he could see little Pooch wagging his tail with a sparkle in his eyes. He didn't know who ate the hamburgers the fastest, the old man or the little dog. He got the biggest delight in helping the old man and the little dog that morning.

The old man took a sip of the hot coffee and held it up and said, "Thank you for the coffee. We must be on our way." Jeff stood there a couple of minutes watching the two fade out of sight, crossing the railroad track bridge heading toward the old courthouse, up Highway 41 North.

He said over forty years later, he still gets much delight bringing back those memories and the characters along the way. He often wonders, all these years later, whatever happened to the old man and Pooch. He hoped and prayed that the old man and dog got to spend the rest of their days together traveling around and being free. After all, being free is having nothing to lose!

THE SINGING SHERIFF

Don Page, a Sumter County deputy, was elected the sheriff of Sumter County.

Don had previously worked for longtime Sumter County sheriff, Fred Roselle. Fred had been sheriff for approximately twenty years and lived in Wahoo, Florida, in Sumter County. Jeff really liked Sheriff Roselle. He was a quiet Southern gentleman, and you never saw him without that white cowboy hat, which was somewhat of a tradition back in the day. A lot of the sheriffs wore those white Stetson hats.

Changing times saw the old traditions slowly fade away, somewhat like the color of the Florida Sheriff's patrol cars. About 1972, all the sheriffs' cars were white with a four-inch green stripe along the front and back fenders. That also slowly faded away, and the color scheme today is all different, still white with green but with different designs. In my opinion, the sheriff's association should have kept the same paint scheme on all the Florida Sheriff's cars, somewhat like the Florida Highway patrol cars. However, as time moved on, so did old traditions. New sheriffs were being elected from the north. They brought their ideas to Florida with them. Tradition meant nothing anymore!

Now back to the singing sheriff.

Don Page had lived in Sumter County most of his life and served in the Marine Corp and fought in the Korean War before going into law enforcement. When Don took office, Sumter County was a rural county with a population of about seven thousand people. Don was also a country musician and singer. One of his songs appeared on the soundtrack of the original *Walking Tall* movie starring Joe Don Baker in 1973.

Jeff told me personally he liked Don and that he had met him early on in his career as sheriff. He also told me Don Page seemed to be a fair-minded fellow and was easy to talk to. Jeff further stated his opinion was that Don was much better as a musician than most.

Jeff said when he went to Sumter County as a deputy after leaving Hernando County in 1984, he was hired by Sheriff Jamie Adams and enjoyed working for Sheriff Adams, whom he had known from being a game warden. Jamie Adams was a great sheriff and made many changes during his years as sheriff.

Jeff also said one evening about 1985 that his youngest son Avery was riding with him on the late shift. Don Page, after being defeated by Jamie Adams, was appointed police chief in Center Hill, Florida, a one-man department. Page called Jeff on the Sumter County band and asked Jeff to meet him in Center Hill. Jeff figured he just wanted to chat, have someone to talk to.

When Avery and Jeff met Page in Center Hill, it was a cool night. The officers met door-to-door so they could talk with the windows down. Jeff and Avery enjoyed the stories the ole singing sheriff told them that evening. After about forty-five minutes, Jeff told Page he had to get back and check some other areas on this patrol duty.

As they drove away, young Avery, said, "He's quite a character."

His daddy replied, "Yes, he is. He's a good ole boy and I can't help but feel a little sorry for him. He let his personal problems and other issues get in the way of his career and that is what ended his career."

Don Page slowly faded away from law enforcement. He succumbed to his vices and became very ill and died in 1989 and was buried in his beloved Sumter County.

STUCK ON I-95 IN CUBA

Bufford T. Justice played the sheriff in *Smokey and the Bandit*, and that's a fact. It was a very funny movie.

As Jeff and I sat at the breakfast table one morning, he shared with me one of the funniest stories in his long career as a law enforcement officer. Before we get into the story itself, I suppose we all know that Burt Reynolds was a Florida native and played football at FSU in Tallahassee. Jeff was very fond of Burt. He also relayed to me that he had worked personally for Jerry Reed, the famous "Alabama Wild Man" singer and songwriter, as he called himself in one of his songs, who also costarred in *Smokey and the Bandit* with Burt Reynolds. Jeff was fortunate enough to have worked security for Jerry Reed at a performance in the 1980s and was able to sit and talk with Jerry on his private bus for several hours. He said Jerry was a "watch you see is what you get" kind of guy. Now all this somewhat tie together the story I'm going to tell you.

The story starts in 1976 when Sheriff Melvin Kelly sent Jeff to Homestead, Florida, to deliver a prisoner to the federal prison. The family of a young inmate requested that Jeff be the transporting officer since they had known him since childhood. He had agreed to take the assignment on his day off without pay.

This was along about the time that gasoline and automobiles were having an estranged relationship due to the fact the vehicles were being produced with catalytic converters. Jeff told me the sheriff, being the hardheaded Irishman he was, found himself in somewhat of a pickle, because some of the older patrol cars were still being run on leaded gas that they still used to fill their tanks at the old sheriff's office. The new ones would only run on unleaded gas because of the catalytic converters.

He said he walked into the sheriff's office to talk to the sheriff about the trip. He brought up the fact his new Chevrolet patrol car would not perform on unleaded gas and told the sheriff he could probably get to Homestead and would have to refuel on the way back with unleaded fuel. He knew it would damage the car but did not know exactly how or what would happen. The hardheaded sheriff was having no part of this. He knew he could not argue with Melvin Kelly because once he made up his mind, that is the way it was going to be.

The sheriff's last words were, "Just fill it up anyway and come on back."

Since he was the man with the golden badge, he replied, "Okay, Mel, you got it."

Jeff said it was a nice trip down. He had known the young inmate and his family since he was a little boy. He hated to see the young man go to federal prison but also knew he had to pay the price for the crimes he had committed. Once he dropped Timmy off, he dreaded the long trip back but hit I-95 in good spirits heading north toward Miami.

In 1976, he said everybody had a CB radio. The craze was rampant. Most all the deputies in Hernando County had one in their patrol car. They were used mostly to listen to people on the road bragging about their speed and where the Smokey's were. If a law enforcement officer would listen, you could figure out about where they were, and it would aid in catching drug traffickers, reckless drivers, and speeders.

He did admit that occasionally, he enjoyed having a little fun, being the character he was, with the CB radio! His handle was "Bull of the Woods." Curtis Coral had a CB in his patrol car, and his handle was "Green Wheels." John Whitman had a CB in his patrol car and his handle was "Rubber Duck." Now, Jeff was known to change his handle sometimes daily or on the spur of the moment and disguise his voice as a character fitting his mood and location. Sometimes he would come back to somebody, and he would be the "Black Snake."

Some of the other characters were "the Green Monster," "Buck Shot," and some that he could not mention; but he always had fun every chance he got.

He said as he headed north out of Homestead, cruising along in his new Chevrolet, not listening to his two-way, but listening to his CB radio, enjoying the people along I-95 chatting about the county-mounty headed north. He said he was running about 75 mph and slowly began to realize that the Chevrolet was slowing, slowing, slowing down as cars began to line up behind him. They hesitated to pass a marked patrol car. He thought to himself, *What the heck is going on? It's only going 65 mph, and I haven't taken my foot off the gas.* He looked in the rearview mirror, and the line was getting longer, and the new Chevrolet was getting slower. Then it hit him, like a flash of lightning—the unleaded gas was coming into play. Little did he know what was going to happen next.

As he rolled north going even slower, the car finally leveled out at 35 mph, with his foot on the floor. Now, this wasn't so funny to Jeff. He remembered telling that hardheaded Irishman of a sheriff, the car would not operate properly. Now it was his butt that was stuck on I-95, coming into Miami, Florida, where nobody spoke English.

He could hear the people behind him on their CBs talking about the county-mounty running north and running radar slowly up I-95. He thought, *Running radar is the last thing on my mind.*

He pulled into a Shell Gas Station. Back in those days, the attendant would come out and pump the gas, clean your windshield, and check your oil. He decided to get out of his patrol car because he knew he was going to have trouble getting the attendant to pump the leaded gas, which they still had some, in this new unleaded car.

He got out of the car and spoke to the man approaching his car from the station. He said, "Fill it up, please," as the attendant walked around the car. The man took the pump handle and tried to put it in the gas tank, but it would not fit. Surprise! Now, the attendant was of Cuban descent and did not speak one word of English. Now Jeff was a Florida cracker and only spoke a few words of Spanish; a young

Mexican girl named Tina had taught him, and it sure wasn't about putting gas in a car!

At this point, he asked the attendant if he spoke any English. The attendant replied, "*No speakada Engla.*" Jeff told me he looked at him and thought, *Oh, what am I going to do now? Here I am stuck in Little Havana out of gas. I might as well be in a foreign country. Now, how am I going to get home?*

After a few choice words that the attendant did not understand—and that's probably a good thing because they included things he could not write in this book—he jerked the pump nozzle out of the attendant's hand and began filling the car with leaded gas. He paid the attendant and pulled back onto I-95 in a fast manner as he was mad, mad, mad of the whole damn situation.

He said he was speeding north at a blazing 35 mph, listening to the people behind him starting to slow down because the county-mounty was back on the interstate running radar again. He began to laugh. He said, "If they only knew the jokes on them. I'm going to enjoy this day one way or another. It's going to be a long time getting home."

He began to figure what time in the morning he would arrive home, doing 35 mph. Normally, it would be about an eight-hour drive, but at this rate it would take about sixteen hours to get back to Brooksville, but as I said earlier, he was a survivor.

He began to listen closely to the traffic behind him and heard someone calling a guy with the handle, "the Toy Hauler." Now, he wondered what the Toy Hauler was. He was tired of telling people he was not running radar and called the Toy Hauler on the CB. "Bull of the Woods to the Toy Hauler, come back." He didn't know exactly how far this little CB would go. He knew the Toy Hauler had to be close because he heard him yakking with other CBers. Again, he broke radio silence. "Bull of the Woods to the Toy Hauler, what's your 10-20?"

"Toy Hauler. Go ahead Bull."

"Bull of the Woods back to the Toy Hauler."

"I'm that county-mounty that everybody is talking about."

"You're kidding!"

"No, sir, I'm not kidding. What are you hauling?"

The Toy Hauler replied, "Dead, heading back to Wildwood. I'm a tractor hauler."

"Bull of the Woods back to the Toy Hauler, when you pass me, pull over into the emergency lane and stop in front of me. I need to talk to you. I need some help."

"10-4, good buddy!"

He was delighted to say the least that someone was willing to help him. He saw a ray of light as the Toy Hauler passed and began to pull over in the emergency lane of I-95 about fifteen miles north of Miami, Florida.

The two stopped and got out of their vehicle, and Jeff approached the truck driver. At this point in his life, he was a little pudgy, kind of like Buford T. Justice, but not quite as big. With a uniform on and a hat, he kind of reminded himself of the actor, especially with that hat he hated to wear so much. He began to explain his misfortune to the truck driver and asked if he could haul him in his patrol car as far north as Wildwood.

The truck driver replied, "Anything to help you out. I'll be happy to."

Jeff said, "Let the ramps down on that truck, and I'll drive this Chevrolet right up on that flatbed tractor hauler."

"Okay, you're the boss!"

He told him that when he got back on I-95, to let the hammer down, northbound. "I will have my blue lights on and CB radio as we head north."

As he pulled up on the tractor hauler, he began to laugh. *How funny this must look to the people passing us on I-95.* Once the car was loaded, the ramps came up, and away they went with the blue lights flashing and the CB blasting.

Now ole Jeff had the time of his life, laughing and waving at the folks as they looked up and laughed and waved back. What a hoot! He wasn't mad at the ole sheriff anymore. He was having the time of his life, waving and talking to the folks on the CB radio. He was just being Jeff Duval.

When he arrived and met with the sheriff the next day, he told Sheriff Kelly, "Don't ever send me back to Dade County. No one speaks English, Mel, and they sure don't speak Southern American."

TWO LOST TRAVELERS

Jeff told me a story of two travelers that he had met early Easter morning in 1980, just after sunrise. The travelers were hitchhiking north about eight miles out of town.

Back then, it was customary to stop and check travelers out and to do a field investigation report (FIR) to see if they were wanted or had a record. Also, if something came up later, it would show the travelers were in the area at that time.

As Jeff slowly approached the two travelers, he realized the taller one looked a little less road weary, and the second guy was smaller in stature and a little more road worn. He advised the two men he needed to see some identification. The taller man had a government retirement card from the air force and a Florida driver's license. The other fella only had a Social Security card. He ran their names through the computer. Neither one came back wanted or with a record.

Jeff said he stepped out of the patrol car into the cool, crisp morning air. He noticed the smell of alcohol on the smaller man. The taller fella smelled a little cleaner and seemed to be more educated as Jeff began to watch their body language. One thing you always did as an officer was watch body language. He could tell the taller man was a little more comfortable talking to him. He asked him what he did for a living. The taller man said he was retired from the air force and had been a little down on his luck lately. He believed the man was telling the truth. When he questioned the shorter fella, he was just a road traveler and alcoholic. He then asked the men where they were headed. They told him they were headed to Northwest Florida, close to Pensacola, and thought they would travel together because it would be safer.

The two men told Jeff they had been traveling for about four days and nights from down South. He told me that he felt compassion for the two men because it was shortly after sunrise on Easter morning. Usually, when he was off work, he would attend sunrise service at Chinsegut Hill on Easter morning with his family. Jeff also said as a law enforcement officer, you very seldom had a holiday off.

He said he asked the two men when the last time they had eaten. The retired air force man said it had been a couple of days since they had a real meal. He said he then asked them if they knew what today was. Neither of the men remembered it was Easter morning. Jeff reached into his pocket and pulled out the only money he had, a $20 bill. Usually, he said he didn't have that much money in his pocket, but he felt compelled to give the money to the lost travelers.

When he handed the $20 to the airman, he just stared at the money and said, "Do you want to give us the $20?"

Jeff said, "Yes, that's all I have." He knew that he could go home to a well-prepared Easter meal.

The two men began to thank him for the money. He said he told the two travelers it was up to them how they spent the money, even though he had given it to them to buy something to eat, not to drink. The smaller guy said, "Thank you so much. No officer has ever given me anything."

Jeff thought this was a very appropriate time to say, "Don't thank me. This is Easter morning, the day the good Lord rose from the tomb so we may have everlasting life. Remember this day and remember the good Lord gave you this and only used me as a vessel to pass it along to you." He said they told him they would buy food and put it to good use. He looked at the two and could see a tear run down the retired airman's cheek. Jeff shook their hand and watched them walk north on Highway 98 and hoped the good Lord would watch over them in their travels.

As he looked around before stepping back in his patrol car, he saw the brilliant sun rising from the east and said, "Thank you, Lord, for using me this morning."

BUBBA GOES TO EUROPE

....

Now Bubba was not your average deputy sheriff. He was born in the South of course. He was well educated and liked the Southern living style and liked being who he was, somewhat a character. He was known for his old-time ways of thinking and doing his job sometimes. He would tell you what he thought about things and look you straight in the eye when he talked serious.

I had occasion to witness him talking to a young thief one day in a parking lot. It was a chance encounter. Bubba had locked him up several times for stealing and being a thief. The young man was quite large. Bubba was stout but wasn't that tall. The thief could be a smart ass. He walked up to Bubba and said, "Hey, Deputy Bubba, somebody is going to kill your ass one of these days."

Bubba's reply was "You wanna kill me, big man?"

"I damn sho' do."

With that, Bubba began being Bubba. He pulled that big .44 Smith & Wesson Magnum, twirled it once like Roy Rogers, spun it butt up, and shoved it toward the thief. And to my amazement, he said, "Here, asshole, put me out of my misery."

The big thief was so scared that he stepped back, eyes and mouth wide open, and said, "You're crazy, man. You damn sho' real crazy!" Maybe Bubba was or Bubba had the nads and knew the big man didn't!

Sometimes he would remind you of ole Willie Post! He just wanted people to think he was a little crazy. Some of the things he did would make you think he was too! Occasionally, he would make you think of the movie *Walking Tall.* He was a little like Buford Pusser, sheriff of McNairy County, Tennessee. Bubba sure did not back up.

Well, about 1985, he said that he and some friends decided to take a trip to Europe for two weeks. He had always heard how good the German beer was by one of his cousins that had been in the army over there. Gene Harris, up in Panama City, Florida, had been stationed in Germany for two years. Now ole Gene was kind of rough cut, a millwright at the International Paper Company in Panama City. Back in the day, he would have been what you would call a man's man. That's where Bubba got some of his swagger, hanging around ole Gene when he was a kid. He said ole Harris was like Superman to him!

When Bubba got on that big jumbo jet at Tampa International Airport, it was just getting dark. He was off on an adventure of a lifetime. As the plane ascended, you could hear the big engines roar, lifting into the night sky. As it turned across Tampa Bay, you could see the city of Tampa below. What a beautiful sight. Bubba wondered if he would ever see home again. He knew a lot of things could happen on this adventure and they did. Some real surprises lay ahead. The flight was approximately nine hours to Frankfort, West Germany, with a stop off at Heathrow Airport, in London, England.

The flight over was long and boring. Daylight came after two or three hours into the flight because they were flying toward the sun. Bubba thought that was a short night, not much sleep. The jumbo jet glided into Heathrow without incident. It was daytime again after a short night.

After a layover at Heathrow, they boarded a small jetliner heading for Frankfort, West Germany. After a short flight, the pilot came on audio to say, "May I have your attention, please. We will soon be descending into Frankfort, West German Airport. Please be advised, you do not have any civil rights in Germany. If you are approached by the military or police, do as you are instructed without question." He thought, *Wow! You do not want to make these guys mad.* He hadn't thought about such things but realized the seriousness of being in another country. There was a lot to be learned in the days ahead.

As he departed, he looked to his right and saw a large Russian airliner sitting next to them on the tarmac. When he saw that arm and hammer on the tail wing of that big jet, he said to himself, *I ain't in Oz anymore*, and felt a little uneasy as they walked into the airport. He noticed several German police officers or military men walking around with semiautomatic and automatic rifles. He knew he was in a strange place because you would not see this in an American airport.

He and his friends caught a cab and went to the hotel where they would be staying in Frankfort. It was a beautiful old building with lots of granite and grandeur. After Bubba slept for about an hour, he told his buddies he couldn't wait to get out before dark and start his new adventure. After getting cleaned up and showering, ole Bubba hit the streets. He and his friends decided to go their separate ways.

He decided, after arriving in Frankfort, the first thing he needed to do was have some coffee and breakfast. The waiter was a well-dressed young German fella. He noticed the white towel he had over his arm. Now, Bubba being a Southerner always had grits with his breakfast. He asked the young man for two eggs over medium, and knowing they didn't have biscuits, he ordered toast and a side of grits. The young German looked at him very sternly and said, "What is a grit?" Bubba couldn't help but laugh, thinking about them Yankees from the Bronx and them stopping along the roadside to pick some grits on the way to Disney World.

He told his friends he couldn't wait to taste that German beer he had heard about from his friends in the military from years before. It was beginning to get dark when Bubba looked up the street and thought that must surely be a tavern. There were young people hanging around the neon sign over the sidewalk. He said, "Surely this must be a tavern." As he approached them, he noticed something very strange to his American eyes. In America, you did not see people with three-quarters of their head shaved, especially on a girl, and the rest of the hair braided down her back. The girl had more metal in her face than a D-8 Caterpillar with leather wrist bands and spikes on her wrist, high-top leather boots, and two or three friends that looked even more weird. He began to think this must be one strange bar. You might get your clock cleaned in here without a gun, but he was not one to back up. He was looking for an adventure.

He noticed a dark steep stairwell going up at least one floor to a flat with a desk. As he approached the desk, he saw a large man with a turban. There were a lot of people from Afghanistan and Iraq in West Germany, but Bubba thought, *That rag is piled high enough to clean the ceiling fixtures.* The big man had a face full of hair. He wondered where he kept his large knife. He just exchanged his money that afternoon and had no idea how much money he had in his pocket. All he knew was that it was German. Bubba looked down on the desk and saw a large hardback book with lots of names, so he figured he had to register to get in.

He looked the big Afghan in the eye and said with a motioning gesture, "I would like to go into the bar and have a beer." He looked quickly to the left and saw a small glass window. The bar was dimly lit. He could hear people laughing, and the music playing, and it seemed like they were having a good time. He then gestured again to the Afghan, "I would like to go in and have a beer," and held out a few German coins to show them to the big dude behind the desk. He looked back at Bubba with a somewhat unfriendly look and said, "*Nein.*" Bubba knew that meant no in German. He had studied a little bit of the German language before making the trip over. There were certain key words he wanted to know. Now, you've got to realize Bubba's attire was not what you would call the standard German dress. He was wearing a pair of old pointer bib overalls with a Florida State Jersey underneath and a pair of brown cowboy boots, of course! The big Afghan looked a little startled at his appearance. Bubba once again held out more coins and thought maybe he hadn't found the right money yet and jestered once again to the big man that he wanted to drink a beer and have a little fun. Well, ole "Turban Head" wasn't having none of it. "*Nein.*" Bubba thought, *Dang*, and pulled out some paper money. At which time, the big Afghan said, "*Gay ba*," and stood up and looked up and down at Bubba's boots, bib overalls, and that FSU Jersey up close. Now Bubba had no clue what kind of German money a "*Gay ba*" was.

He and the Afghan were beginning to get a little agitated at each other, but he was determined to have a German beer and said, "I hope you don't understand English, you big jackass." All he wanted was to go inside and have a damn beer and have a little fun, but he could tell that the big fella was really getting perturbed as he stood up, leaned back, and said slowly, "Gay ba." Now Bubba was not quick on what this fella was trying to say, kind of like in the movie *Cool Hand Luke*. "What we have hea is a failya to communicate," but it slowly began to ooze into his brain like cane syrup running off a buttermilk cathead biscuit. "Dang, he's trying to tell me this is a gay bar." With that, Bubba let out a yell and start running down the steps knocking down them weirdos standing on the sidewalk at the bottom of the steps. He started stepping high down the street yelling, "Wait, help! I done got in a gay bar! Come back! Get me out of here! That Afghan guy likes me." He ran until he was out of breath but caught up with his friends. He was never so glad to see anybody in his life. When Bubba told them about his crazy experience in the "gay ba," they all burst out laughing. That will teach you, you crazy cracker.

Well, after strolling around and finding a beer or two, he was sampling different brands and found some were better than others. One thing he learned—Germans do not drink their beer real cold, just cool. He thought that must give them a buzz quicker.

Another thing he noticed was that a lot of women did not shave their legs or underarms. A lot of the younger girls were shaved. Bubba really didn't care whether they had a little hair or not. If they were built right and pretty, he could deal with it. "Oh well, enough of that." Most of them were very beautiful girls, but overall he did not find where the Germans were overly friendly to the Americans.

In the next few days, he made his way over into Switzerland and Austria. When they crossed the checkpoint, just a line in the road, two guards with machine guns checked their passports, and then they could proceed into Switzerland. They found the Swiss people to be very different. They were very friendly and loving people. He spent the first night in a lodge on top of a huge mountain glacier. The water that came out of tap was like ice water, and the view from the lodge was so spectacular with the wind blowing the snow over the glacier top.

The next morning, Bubba went jogging in the Swiss Alps, with a beautiful brunette with blue eyes. He will never forget jogging with

Sherry in the Swiss Alps. There were trails all through the mountains for many miles. It was so beautiful in the springtime, and it was heavenly. The grass was so green with big patches of snow in low spots as you jog along. You could hear the cowbells in the distance, and the farmers did not have any fences. The farmers kept track of their cows by putting a different sounding bell on each animal. That's how they kept track of their herd. He thought, *What a wonderful heavenly place.* The air was so crisp and clean. All the trees were very small, and you had a spectacular view everywhere you went. They came upon a chalet up in the mountains. The Swiss people would not let them buy anything when they found out they were Americans. They had cheese and beer and whatever they wanted. The people would not accept any money and did not want them to leave, but they finally made their way, walking back down to the lodge. He hated to see the day come to an end.

They then made their way over into Austria. The people were the same there as they were in Switzerland. After taking a cruise down the Rhine River and being out of his environment for two weeks, he was ready to get home.

The trip over to Europe was long and boring. On the way, back Bubba decided that he wasn't going to be bored. Damn the torpedos, full speed ahead!

After a gorgeous young stewardess came over and asked him if he wanted a drink, he said, "Yes, ma'am, I think I will have Jack Daniel's, straight up." After about two of these, Bubba decided to stand up and stretch his legs and walked up to the bar where the two stewardesses were tending the bar. After about two hours talking to these two young ladies, who were now giving Bubba free drinks, he wasn't feeling any pain, and he sure as heck wasn't bored. One of the young stewardesses asked him if he would like to live in Miami with her in her apartment. She knew he was a deputy sheriff and must have felt he would be a good roommate and bodyguard. He told her he would talk to her later about that. He didn't know how long he stood there and talked to these gorgeous girls, but they sure had a fun trip back.

When Bubba got back to his seat, three or four older ladies began to chat. One of the ladies asked him if he would help them carry their wine off the plane when they landed in Tampa. He, being the Southern gentleman he was, couldn't say no to these lovely old ladies, but he didn't realize each one of these ladies had three or four jugs of wine on a rope until they loaded him down like a pack mule as they were getting off the plane.

It was a very delightful trip back across the Pacific. When Bubba got off the plane in Tampa, he actually got down on his knees and kissed the runway and said, "Thank you, Lord, for bringing me back to the USA."

But one of the funniest things occurred to Bubba later the next day. "Germany did not have one damn grit."

We have no idea how blessed we are to live in the United States of America, home of the free, land of the brave. I would like to thank those who serve(ed) in the armed forces overseas. May God bless them all for their sacrifices.

DIZZY BLOND TRIES POSSUM TRICK

In 1988, Jeff had been hired at the Gulf County Sheriff's Office by Sheriff Harrison. He was given the rank of lieutenant, third in command.

Jeff shared a funny little story with me that occurred in Gulf County in the fall of 1993. One morning about one thirty, his phone rang at home, which was not unusual. When he answered the phone, the dispatcher advised she had a patch through from one of the deputies on the road. We will just call him Hooch for namesake.

Deputy Hooch said, "I have your sister stopped on the new high-rise bridge over the intercoastal waterway."

Jeff asked, "Why are you calling me?"

Hooch replied, "What do you want me to do with her?"

He replied, "Do what you have to do. You don't have to ask me just because she's my sister."

Hooch's reply was "Good night, Lieutenant. 10-4."

Jeff told me he had dozed back off to sleep, and the phone rang again about two thirty. "Deputy Hooch wants to talk to you again, Lieutenant," and was patched through.

Hooch said, "Sir, I hate to wake you up again, but I have your sister again coming down the high-rise bridge on a riding lawnmower on the cityside."

Jeff knew his younger sister well and knew she had a little bit of a wild streak. With her looks, with the long blonde hair and blue eyes, she had a way of talking herself out of trouble most of the time. When he asked Hooch what she was doing to get stopped,

Hooch's reply was "She is driving the lawnmower again and has been drinking."

Jeff replied, "Well, dang. Is she pulling the possum in a wagon behind her?" remembering the story of the country music singer doing the same thing.

Hooch asked, "What do you want me to do with her?"

Being lieutenant came before being a brother. Jeff replied, "If it was me, I would lock her up. I have never told my men not to arrest. That is at your discretion. It doesn't matter who it is but don't call me again tonight. You do your job." Jeff after hanging up the phone went back to bed and asleep.

The next day, after getting all his office duties taken care of, the first thing Jeff wanted to do was drive to his sister's house. When he arrived, he saw her out in the yard working on her flowers. When he stepped out of his unmarked car and walked over, she looked a little frightened. He said, "Well, sis, I heard you played possum and had a big-time last night. Where did you get the idea of riding a tractor mower to town?"

She looked a little dazed and said with a chuckle, "Yeah, I thought I would try what ole George Jones did. I always liked his music, and with a little too much to drink, I just got on the tractor mower to go have another drink at the St. Joe Bar."

Jeff said, "Listen, sister, I believe in having fun as much as the next person, but there is a limit to anything. You can't be riding around on a lawnmower or a car while you are drinking. You know better. Don't expect me to treat you any different than any other citizen when it comes to obeying the law. Do you understand me?"

She looked up at Jeff with those beautiful blue eyes and said, "Yes, big brother, I understand." With that she gave her brother a hug.

He turned around and walked toward the patrol car and stopped and looked back and said, "Dang, that sure was funny though."

While driving back to the sheriff's office downtown, he reminisced about all the good times they had in their younger days when they would go floundering around in her boat. She was good at gigging and catching fish in the gulf, especially flounder. Jeff had six sisters and was the only son of his daddy. He loved them all very much. Her being the baby girl, she had always been spoiled, and Jeff had tried to keep her on the right path but knew she would have to grow out of that little wild streak and hoped time would take care of it.

That afternoon, he had what he used to call a prayer meeting with Deputy Hooch.

STANDING EYE TO EYE WITH DEATH

• • • • • • • • • • • • •

One Friday morning started off like any other day. I picked up the mic in my patrol car and said, "11 Brooksville 10-8." I arrived at the sheriff's office about six o'clock, gassed up my patrol car, and went into the office to get a cup of coffee. I checked the night radio log, like I always do, to see what happened the night before so we would be informed of what was going on during the prior twelve-hour shift. It was protocol back in those days. I then went to briefing, talked to the guys a minute, and then hit the road.

As I pulled out of the parking lot, I was wondering what new adventure this rookie would experience today. One thing was sticking in my mind from the night radio log. John Darnman and his wife had another fight the prior evening. I remembered them from being dispatched to their home several times in the last few weeks. John was a truck driver hauling locally, and his wife Julie was a waitress at the L&M Truck Stop. Most locals called it the greasy spoon, about six miles north of Brooksville, on Highway 98. John was known to be a tough guy and would sometimes get hopped up on pills or maybe alcohol. I had always been able to handle him before without a tussle, but this day was going to be different.

The owner of the truck stop was a beautiful brunette girl with big blue eyes by the name of Chrissy. Sometime around midmorning, the truck stop was full of truck drivers and rock miners having lunch. At which time, John was in town at the local hardware store, buying a .38 Smith & Wesson and a box of shells.

I was in the office talking to dispatch when all hell broke loose. All three radios, FHP, innercity frequency, and the sheriff's band, were all a buzzing. From what the dispatcher and I could determine, there had been a shooting at the L&M Truck Stop. Chief Deputy Melvin Kelly and three other deputies sped north to the scene of the shooting.

It was later revealed by witnesses that John had walked in about lunchtime, when he knew Julie would be working. John had the .38 in his back pocket hidden by his shirttail. Julie saw him drive up and ran into the storeroom to hide.

John calmly walked over to the register and lunch counter where he was met by Chrissy, the pretty brunette who owned the truck stop and who was also a close friend of Julie's, and said, "I want to see my wife."

Chrissy replied, "John, don't start any trouble. We are really busy."

John was standing right in front of Chrissy at the register. He pulled the .38 out of his back pocket and fired the fatal shot, striking Chrissy between the eyes. Blood and brain matter hit the wall behind her. The customers didn't have a clue of what was going on until the shot was fired. Someone called the sheriff's office. People were running and climbing out of windows to try and escape the scene.

Chief Kelly, Deputy Richard Clay, and two other deputies rolled north out of Brooksville to the scene, along with Sheriff Lowman. They were joined by Florida Highway Patrol, Lieutenant Bill Lloyd, and two other state troopers, who had been working the area for several years. John took his wife Julie, rushed out the back door to get away, and didn't remember he had left the bullets in his car, which was parked out front of the truck stop. He only had five bullets left, but the law enforcement officers didn't know this at the time. John forced his wife into the truck stop owner's pink Cadillac and made Julie drive away by holding the gun to the temple of her head as they sped from the scene. A little later, John remembered that the box of .38 bullets was in his car back at the truck stop. He told his wife, "Let's go back and get the box of shells out of my car." Julie turned around and drove back to the truck stop. It was clear at that point he meant to kill more people.

John didn't realize that the sheriff, deputies, and highway patrol were arriving at the scene when they pulled into the parking lot. No more bullets were to be had. When John saw the officers and Chief Deputy Melvin Kelly, the bullets started flying. John shot first, and then the officers started firing back. Chief Deputy Kelly put three carbine holes in the pink Cadillac, two in the trunk and one in the back glass, shattering it. None of the officers were hit at the scene of the shoot-out.

Deputy Richard Clay and Deputy Danny Spencer were left to guard the scene. The sheriff and the lieutenant from the Florida Highway Patrol, a trooper, and a Citrus County deputy followed the pink Cadillac southward toward Brooksville.

I sped north to see if I could assist and saw what looked like a small parade coming up Stringer Hill toward me. I was a green rookie and couldn't believe what was happening. I pulled my patrol car off to the right side of Highway 98 at Stringer Hill. For a second, it was like I was a little kid watching a parade go by. The next second reality hit me, seeing John holding that pistol to Julie's head making her drive toward Brooksville. I spun the car around and joined the parade of law enforcement officers to do whatever I could to help. Julie wasn't speeding, just driving as if she were on a normal Sunday drive. I was wondering what she must be thinking driving, with that pistol being pressed to her head knowing that her husband had just killed her best friend back at the truck stop.

Julie's mother and her children were at her mother's house, just east of Brooksville. Julie's mother lived on Thrill Hill off Neff Lake Road. The sheriff had ordered two deputies to get the children out of the house and to a safe place, because he figured that might be where John was headed.

John forced Julie to pull into the Tiki Hut, a local bar on the east side of town near the city limits. John had her pull the Cadillac up to the front door, longways. We all pulled off Highway 50 East and waited to see what was going down next. We didn't dare try a move with all the innocent people in the line of fire. I'm thinking he needed more liquid courage. John told the waitress in the Tiki Hut to get him a pack of cigarettes and a bottle of Jack Daniel's. The pink Cadillac pulled out of the Tiki Hut, leaving a bunch of good ole boys sitting at the bar and the waitress staring out the front door, shaking and sweating with all the law enforcement following John and Julie east. At this time, we knew where he was going, to Julie's mother's house. With his liquid courage and a pack of smokes, he was ten feet tall and bulletproof. I knew then it wasn't going to be as easy for me to deal with him as it had been in the past.

Sheriff Lowman called Florida Highway Patrol, Lieutenant Bill Lloyd, and said, "Bill, take your troopers and come in the back and go around the other side of Thrill Hill, out of sight." The sheriff knew John would be blocked in with all the deputies on this side and all the troopers on the other side of the pink Cadillac. Sure enough, John went straight to Julie's mother's house right on top of Thrill Hill. They pulled right up to the front of the house on the grass, thinking that the grandmother and the children would be in the house. I knew that the liquor had to be working on this killer by now.

I rolled to a stop just behind the sheriff's big green Buick. Other Hernando County deputies and deputies from the surrounding counties were pulling up behind me. I looked to my left and saw Bill Brayton loading his M1 carbine, with a full clip. At this moment in time, it became surreal—one of us, John, or Julie might die today. I remember the sheriff saying, "Try and get a shot on him." Time came to a standstill for me. Everything seemed to be moving in slow motion.

In my mind, I was just a young rookie. It bothered me to run over a small animal or dog. Now the sheriff was telling me to kill a man that I knew. I knew that he had just killed a beautiful young girl. I was looking at him holding a gun to his wife's head. At this point in time, it became abundantly clear what the job of law enforcement is all about.

I knew that I had to try something else first. I knew John but realized he was a killer now. I pulled my carbine up on him with a fully loaded thirty-round clip. I didn't know if I could pull the trigger or not, as I slid my finger onto the trigger. Everyone was trying to get an angle on him.

Julie was sitting behind the steering wheel, screaming and blowing the car horn the entire time. I knew she had to be in shock. I noticed a fellow deputy and my best friend, Cliff Batten, had pulled his unmarked Chevrolet over to the right side of the road and was squatting behind the right front fender of his car.

In the early 1970s, there were no SWAT teams or negotiators. Deputies had to handle these types of situations as best they could. I believed that day if anyone was going to save Julie's life, it had to be me, a scared young rookie. I knew both John and Julie and didn't want anyone to die that day. I was standing beside the sheriff's car and asked him if he would let me talk to John since I had dealt with him before with other domestic problems. The sheriff looked at me for a few seconds and said, "Jeff, I can't ask you to do that."

I replied, "Sheriff, let me try to save her. If he takes the gun off her and puts it on me, she can get out of the car and run."

The sheriff took a deep breath and said, "Go ahead."

I yelled, "John, this is Jeff Duval. Do you remember me?"

I knew that being ten feet tall and bulletproof was working on him now. He replied, "Yeah, you son of a bitch, I remember you."

I said, "Can I come up that way in the road and talk to you?"

He replied, "Yes, come on!"

At this point, time became nonexistent to me. I knew that I was moving into the road toward a killer holding a gun to his young wife's head. After getting in the middle of Neff Lake Road where he could see me, the moment became even more surreal as I felt fear that I had never known or could even imagine. I was in a dark world alone with a killer holding a gun in my face. I told him that I would be unarmed. I dropped my gun belt on the road and said, "John, I'm unarmed." At that point, he took the gun away from Julie's head and put the .38 on me. I was beginning to feel cold and alone in a place and time that I had never been. I knew that everyone was around, but somehow it felt like there was no one in the world except me, the killer, and Julie. All I could hear were her screams and that Cadillac horn continuously blowing. I had never been so alone. Even with so many people around and guns pointed in our direction, sweat began running down into my eyes. All I could see was John and that gun pointed straight at me. I was thinking, *Why hasn't she gotten out of the car and tried to run for safety?* I could feel my muscles beginning to quiver. I felt fear a man looking straight in the eye could feel. I heard John yell and jerk the gun quickly to the left for a second saying, "MF, if you stick your head around that fender one more time, I will kill your ass!" I knew he had to be talking to Cliff, because I knew he was somewhere behind me to the right.

As I was talking to John, I was praying to God to show me a way out. I felt like I had been in the middle of the road for hours trying to talk to this man, but there was no talking to a drunk killer. I began thinking about my beautiful wife and two little sons. I knew they had no way of knowing what was going on right now. It seemed to me that I was in a dream state of mind, not able to see or hear things around me any longer. I could feel death near me as John was trying to decide who or how many he wanted to kill today. It was a feeling that over forty years later I still have nightmares about. The fear is just as bad today as it was that day. It never leaves me.

I asked John to throw the car keys out into the yard. He did, and I knew then that whatever happened was going to happen there. I knew some of us were going to die. I had no cover where I was standing and knew that I was going to die right there or while walking away. I knew I had to make a move.

At that point in time, I thought a prayer to God without speaking: *Lord, I pray you show me a door out of here.* Julie was in shock and was not going to make a move or even get out of the car. Just then John said, "Jeff, there is one thing. I would like to see the kids before anything else goes down." I knew then that something was going to happen but did not know what to expect next. I realized then that God had given me a possible way out. I knew the sheriff wasn't going to allow the kids to be put in harm's way, but I also knew that John was high enough that he didn't know that.

I replied, "John, I'm going back up the road to see if the sheriff will let me get the kids so you can talk to them." I remember it like it was this morning, staring down the barrel of John's gun and turning around. I took three steps and heard a single shot. I lunged forward face down in the middle of Neff Lake Road, thinking this is my day, my death. I felt no pain. Then I heard footsteps running up the hill toward us from both directions and realized I wasn't shot. I looked over my left shoulder and saw John's arm hanging out the window of that pink Cadillac. It was then I realized he had been shot. I jumped up and ran toward him, myself being in shock.

As I got to him, the other officers charged in behind me, shoving me into the car door and John's arm. Citrus County Deputy Ray Bozeman was reaching around me and yelling, "Get that damn gun out of his hand, Jeff!" I felt Bozeman reach around and grab the pistol as I rubbed against the killer's arm. I looked into his face and saw his right eye hanging out onto his cheek and five buckshot holes in his face and neck. Someone pulled me backward. I could hear John gurgling and trying to breathe as he was pulled from the car and laid in the grass. It was a strange moment as John lay dying on the green grass of the lawn. I will never be able to explain what I was feeling at that point in time. I didn't want anybody to die that day.

When I was able to look up, I saw my best friend Cliff standing beside me, holding his personal twelve-gauge shotgun. I was in shock and unable to speak. When I was able to gather my thoughts, I asked him, "What happened?" He said he saw the .38 raise slightly as the killer went to cock it to shoot me in the back as I walked away. Cliff had no other choice but to take John out.

The sheriff knew that the twenty-one-year-old rookie had enough this day. He said, "Jeff, take Julie to the hospital in town." As we walked to the car, no words were spoken. As I pulled my patrol car onto Neff Lake Road, I looked over at Julie, and she looked at me and said, "Why did y'all kill my husband?" I couldn't believe the words I was hearing, but I figured she was in deep shock. Not another word was spoken as we drove to Lykes Memorial Hospital in Brooksville, who had already been put on alert. I don't even remember driving but remember arriving at the back entrance of the emergency room, where we were met outside by a friend of mine from high school Vicki. She asked, "Jeff, are you all right?" I shook my head, and she gave me a hug. Vickie said, "I heard what you did today," wiping tears from her eyes.

I left the hospital and drove back to the County sheriff's office. The office was full of law enforcement officers when I walked in. No one was talking. It was an eerie kind of quiet. As I entered the room, everyone was watching me as I walked by. I went around the counter and sat at the desk next to Cliff. He never looked up or acknowledged that anyone was in the room. He just kept working on the report. As I started my report, it all seemed like a dream. However, as I looked around at the silent officers, I knew it wasn't a dream. At some point, I looked over at the man who saved my life and asked, "Are you okay?" He nodded his head yes, never saying a word.

I then drove down to the Buick–Pontiac Dealership, which was owned by my father-in-law Ernie Chatman Sr. and where my wife was working. My wife and mother-in-law were sitting at their desks in the front office. My father-in-law was standing in the doorway of his office. Mom said, "You look pale. Do you know anything about the shootings today?" I told her what happened. My wife looked at me in disbelief. She ran around her desk and hugged me. My mother-in-law, wiping tears away, said, "Don't you ever do anything like that again." Dad walked outside lighting a cigarette, never saying a word.

That night after supper, while putting my two little sons to bed, I hugged my wife and thanked God for opening a door for me that day.

A few days later, I was at the courthouse in town. One of our county commissioners saw me and walked over and said, "Boy, you were lucky the other day."

I replied, "Chuck, there is no such thing as luck. Luck had nothing to do with me living through that day. I lived through that day by the grace of God, and I had a law enforcement brother that did what had to be done. It's all in the job."

Cliff and I were always close friends. I loved him like a brother until the day he died.

The day after the tragic killings, the local newspaper headline read, "Two shot to death. A local unidentified deputy gave himself up as a hostage to save a young mother's life."

I will never forget those three steps.

I CAN'T SAVE YOU BUT THE LORD CAN

....

This story took place after Jeff transferred to Port St. Joe, Gulf County, Florida, in 1988 where the Constitution was signed by his great-great-granddaddy, William P. Duval, the first territorial governor of Florida. He told me he is proud of his family heritage. He was offered a job there as lieutenant, third in command.

He relayed a story to me once about a retaliation shooting. He was called out in reference to a shooting in the north part of the county in Wewahitchka.

It seemed that some strangers had moved into the area of Wewa. Now, the locals around Wewa were somewhat clannish and tight-knit, but most were good people. A family of Mexicans had wandered into town and rented a small house, and some of the young locals did not like this idea of the strangers moving into town.

Big Rudolph Langston was big and bad and a little bit left of centerline, if you know what I mean. He was always looking for trouble and usually found it. This particular night, he got a twelve-gauge shotgun and a carload of friends and rode around until he found the Mexicans at a convenience store in Wewa. The group pulled into the parking lot of the Sac-O-Suds and shot one of the Mexicans down in the parking lot. All hell broke loose, and the shooting began. Little did Langston know, the Mexicans were ready for them. They picked up the wounded Mexican, put him in the car, and called 911 for an ambulance. After the wounded man was transported, the rest of the Mexicans got back in the car and hit the street looking for Langston and his gang.

After about an hour, they were unable to find Rudolph Langston and his gang. They then drove to Langston's house, got out, and started blowing the horn and yelling. At this point, Langston sent a young man out the front door. Unfortunately, he could not speak Spanish. One of the Mexicans on the driver's side took aim at the fella in the yard, approximately twenty-five yards, and cut loose with a twelve-gauge shotgun on him, striking the young man in the gut. Blood began to pour. The young man screamed and ran in panic. Other shots were exchanged, but no one was hit, and the Mexicans made their escape.

Jeff said he arrived in the area looking for the car the Mexicans were driving but was diverted when dispatch advised him a lady had called in and said there was a young man on her front porch banging on the door yelling for help. When the lady opened the door, she saw a young man lying on her doorstep bleeding profusely from the gut area and holding his insides in with his hands.

When Jeff arrived, he ran over to the front porch. The homeowner was kneeling and crying next to the victim. She was very traumatized by the sight, but Jeff said he knew he had to keep a cool head. He asked the young man his name. The young victim was able to answer and was corresponding fairly well with Jeff. He was told an ambulance was on the way, to lie still, and turn over on his back. At this time, several towels were placed on his stomach as pressure was applied to help slow down the bleeding. Jeff said he was thinking to himself, *This kid will never make it to the hospital,* but he tried to stay calm and give as much aid and comfort as he could.

He could tell the loss of blood was having an effect on the young man. He began to think, *What would I want someone to do for me if I were lying here dying?* Jeff asked the young man if he would like for him to pray for him. He said, "Please do. Please help me." At this time, all three began to pray. Jeff then asked him if he knew his Savior Jesus Christ. The young man nodded his head no. Jeff further asked him if he wanted him to say the Sinner's Prayer for him to save his soul if he didn't make it to the hospital. The young man nodded yes. The young man gave his heart to the Lord while he was lying there bleeding, thinking he was going to die.

The first responders arrived a few minutes after that. and he was transported to Bay Medical Center in Panama City. The long investigation began after meeting with the captain. They found Langston and the gang, and they were taken in for questioning along with the Mexicans. Several arrests were made on both sides.

As time went on, Jeff said he thought about the young man often and wondered if he had died. He had not been notified of a death. Jeff figured the young man had made it through.

Approximately, three months later, Sheriff Harrison called him into the office to have a meeting. At which time, he told Jeff how proud he was for what he had done on the front steps the night he found the young man bleeding and thought he was dying. The sheriff advised Jeff that the family and the victim wanted to meet him at their home. The sheriff shook his hand and said, "Job well done. I'm proud of you. Go see these people when you can find time."

Late that afternoon when things slowed down, Jeff drove to the address where the victim lived and pulled into the driveway and got out and knocked on the door. A young lady answered the door and asked, "Are you Lieutenant Duval?"

Jeff replied, "Yes, ma'am."

"Would you please come into the house?" At which time, she gave him a big hug and said, "We want to thank you for helping to save my brother's life. Had you not been there to apply the pressure with those towels, the doctors said he probably would have bled to death before the ambulance got there."

She turned around and pointed to her right. Jeff saw a tall young man lying in a recliner, bandaged around his torso. The young man held his hand up and motioned for Jeff to come over. The sister told him that this was her brother and he wanted to thank him personally for all that he had done for him that night and opening a door to a new life for him.

He shook his hand and I said, "I am glad that I was there. It was my job to help you. We're here to serve the public and to try and help people in need."

The young man replied, "You did more than help me with my physical ailments. I have a whole new outlook on life because of your prayers and God giving me another chance to be a better person. I will never forget you and neither will my family."

Jeff just smiled and shook his hand and said, "No thanks is necessary."

As he drove away from the home, he felt a sense of calm and joy that the young man had survived and said he would never forget the experience either. He further stated that he always had compassion for people. He said he thought that it was his childhood and the way he was raised that inspired him to help others who are down and was always thankful to God that he could help people in need.

UNDERCOVER

The sheriff called Billy Donn and Grady Dean in his office one Monday morning and said, "Boys, we are going to do some work with the Sarasota County Sheriff's Office. Billy, I'm sending you and Grady down to work on a task force. They're sending us two men to take y'all's place and do some undercover work for us. You two need to report to Major Tony Perez next Monday morning at eight o'clock at the sheriff's office down there." The two were excited about the task force work down South.

The sheriff had obtained the use of a state vehicle that was totally unmarked. It looked more like a cool rod than a law enforcement vehicle, but it was equipped with all the "sneaky pete stuff." The two would be working with a narcotic unit in Sarasota County at night.

The next Monday, Billy Donn and Grady Dean met with Major Perez at eight o'clock at the Sarasota County Sheriff's Office. After the introductions were over, Major Perez called in one of his undercover guys, Phillip Holmes. Phillip looked like he could be a basketball player for the NBA. He was six feet, five inches and was a big boy and a very cordial person. They called him Preacher because he was a part-time Baptist preacher. I couldn't imagine a Baptist preacher working undercover in narcotics, but he knew what he was doing, even though he was young. He took his job very seriously. Now ole Billy Donn was in his glory. He had long black hair and a beard. Grady kind of looked like country singer Eddy Rabbit and was easygoing. He would always follow Billy's lead.

Phillip, being local, had a hot track on this big coke dealer. He said that the bad guy hung around the "Boobie Trap." It was a place in Sarasota County where the girls looked fine "before" closing time, but these girls did look fine before closing time, which ole Billy Donn didn't mind at all since he was a single guy.

Grady knew Billy Donn. As they proceeded, Billy met one of the dancers he really liked. This girl was built like a brick house, very tan, long black hair, and hazel eyes. Billy Donn kept working closer to get to know the girl. He thought maybe he could get some information on the bad guy, if she knew anything about him, and sure enough, she did. She let a few things slip out the next couple of nights. He found out the girl's name was Beth Ann, and she had a boyfriend that was in a biker club that knew the coke dealer. Billy Donn was good at getting information. He looked the part and played the part very well. He kept getting lap dances from Beth Ann. She was taking a liking to Billy. She was giving him free lap dances anytime he wanted them, later in the night, over in the corner of the dimly lit bar. On Thursday night, all three were at the Trap. Billy Donn was getting another lap dance from Beth Ann. Grady and Preacher were sitting at the stage bar. Billy came back over to the bar and told the two guys he was finding out some good info. The chick was really into Billy Donn, but she had told him she was afraid of her boyfriend and his biker buddies. She had told Billy that she would like to spend the night with him but was afraid of Bobby Longhair, her boyfriend.

Beth Ann asked Billy to follow her after work to a hotel in town. He told Preacher and Grady. All three knew of the danger of getting too close to this chick, but Billy Donn wanted to meet her to see what else he could get out of her! Billy told Preacher and Grady to shadow them from a distance and watch the car very closely with some night vision equipment to make sure no one approached the car while he was attempting to obtain more information from Beth Ann. Everything went smoothly. Later that morning, before daylight, Beth Ann dropped Billy off somewhere near their hotel. He did not want her to know where he was staying in case Mr. Longhair found out Beth Ann might be seeing another dude.

The next morning, the three amigos met for breakfast at a local diner in town. Billy and Grady were already there when Preacher walked in with a big smile on his face. As he walked to the booth, he raised his hand up and gave old Billy Donn a high five, and the three men just laughed.

Preacher said, "We could see everything real good Billy until the windows got so foggy, we couldn't see anymore. You are one slick dude, Billy Donn."

Billy knew they had to keep their mind on business at hand. He said, "Guys, all I really got was good information from Beth Ann."

Preacher and Grady just looked at each other and smiled.

The next night, the three returned to the Boobie Trap after a briefing at the sheriff's office with Captain Travis Farmer. The three guys walked in and ordered a beer and sat at the bar where the dancers were performing. The night before, Billy Donn had gotten some good information on this coke dealer from Beth Ann. Billy knew in his mind that the girl was really into him and was giving him information she knew he wanted. He also felt she would not rat him out. He realized the danger of the job, and this was just part of it. Sometimes you had to live on the edge and be careful and not cross the line and lose your life or your job. It was a gamble that the narcotic boys all knew!

Later that night, a Sarasota County deputy sheriff came in the back door to do a walk-around inside. The three guys knew this could blow their entire detail, the deputy not knowing they were working deep under inside the Boobie Trap. Grady looked at Billy Donn and looked very concerned. Billy later admitted that he was on the other side of his own badge; it was a strange feeling. He saw the deputy talking to the manager and was very concerned at this point, because the last couple of nights the manager had been watching them very closely. Billy did not know if the manager had any ties to Beth Ann or her boyfriend, Bobby Longhair, and may have tipped off a deputy he knew about the case. Whatever it may be, it made Billy Donn feel uneasy. Sometimes you go so far under you feel like a bad guy.

Billy was looking straight at the deputy when the worst possible thing happened. The deputy motioned his head for Billy to come to him and the manager. His heart almost stopped. He was thinking he was going to blow the whole thing right there but knew to keep calm and levelheaded. He played it cool and walked over like he was going to talk to the manager.

He said, "Hey, bartender. Can I get a Bud?"

The manager said, "I'm not the damn bartender. I'm the manager."

Billy knew he had to play this just right. He said, "Asshole, I don't care who you are. I just want a beer." He wanted the deputy to jack his ass up in front of everybody, to make it look cool! At which time, the deputy obliged by grabbing Billy and taking him outside. That was the first time Billy had ever been grabbed by a law enforcement officer. He was so relieved when they got out to the alley. There was no one out there but the two of them.

The deputy pushed Billy Donn against the wall and said, "Do you have a driver's license, boy?"

"My driver's license is in my pocket, but you need to call your major at home, and he will verify who I am." Billy added, "Hey, brother man, you fixin' to blow a big case for your sheriff. I'm working undercover in a task force case down here with you guys."

The deputy quickly verified Billy Donn's story and drove away into the night.

To make it look good, he walked back in from the alley. He walked up to the manager, just through inside the back door by the bar, and said in a loud voice, "Now that you've had me shaken down by the cops, can I have my friggin' beer?" The barmaid handed Billy Donn a beer, and he returned to his seat where Preacher and Grady; both were sweating bullets and so was Billy.

Preacher said, "Dang, I can't believe that just happened."

Grady added, "Just carry on like nothing happened, man. We don't want to blow this now. We just come through a tough spot, that's all."

Billy Donn got a lap dance from another girl. *Just to be cool.* Later he told Beth Ann he would see her tomorrow night and would talk to her then. It was getting close to two o'clock in the morning, and the bar would be closing. They had decided Preacher would leave first and then Grady, and he would leave together as they always came in and out together. They made it to their undercover unit without incident. Billy Donn really enjoyed the ride because it was a cool car. A cop car made to look like a hot rod.

As they made their way out of the parking lot, they rode around to make sure no one was tailing them. You sure did not want to relax and forget to use all things you were taught in school and a whole lot of things from experience. A lot of guys have been killed working undercover details like this because they got lax. After driving around for a while, everything looked good, and they made it back to the hotel they were staying at. Billy Donn hit the shower, came out, lay down, and tried to relax for a while. You never knew when the phone would ring or your beeper would go off or when something hot would come in and you would have to take off and go. It must have been around four o'clock in the morning before Billy Donn finally dozed off. About ten o'clock the next morning, the two went to have brunch just outside of town. While sitting at the table, they were discussing the case. Billy Donn told Grady that the girl was getting ready to give him some good information. They drove down to the local Harley Dealership to relax a little. They both loved to ride and had their own motorcycles at home. It was like walking into a candy store when you were a young kid.

Later, the two went back to the room where they changed clothes and called Preacher, who seemed a little edgy for some reason. Billy did not know, but later he would find out. He told Grady he felt like something was bothering Preacher. Grady just smiled and said, "You know how preachers are." They had talked about what time they would meet at the Boobie Trap that night. Billy Donn and Grady would go in about eight forty-five in the evening and get a seat at the bar as the girls would be getting ready to dance on the bar at nine o'clock.

After parking the car, the two strolled in and had a seat at the horseshoe-shaped bar. The girls had gotten to know them well. The first girl to come out was a tall blonde and built like a racehorse. There were no plain janes in this place. They were all young, beautiful ladies. Billy had noticed Grady kind of watching the girls over time. When the dance was over, she leaned over and kissed Grady on the forehead.

When Billy Donn looked at Grady, he laughed and said, "Damn, you sure do have some pretty red lips on your forehead, Grady."

Grady jerked out a handkerchief and wiped it off. "I'm glad you told me. I would hate to walk around like that all night. Some dirtbag would make a crack and piss me off."

The two had a laugh together and had a beer. About that time, Beth Ann strolled over and put her arms around Billy Donn and gave him a kiss on the neck and said, "I want to talk to you later," and asked him if he wanted a lap dance. He looked up at her and smiled, and she knew what that meant. About that time, Preacher came in and strolled over casually, after talking to one of the girls, and sat down by Grady and Billy Donn. Preacher ordered him a beer. He had an odd look on his face. Billy knew something was bothering him and had no earthly idea what was about to happen later that night.

Billy Donn told the guys he was going to take a walk around. Sometimes it was hard for him to sit still. He strolled around the bar thinking he might see the guy they were looking for since they had a better description and a little more information. He made his way back after going in the restroom thinking the guy might be in there but came out empty. As he strolled around, going back to his buddies, he saw Beth Ann nod at him. That meant she wanted to talk to him. He walked over to the guys and told them he was going to get a lap dance. Beth Ann wanted to talk to him. It was hard for Billy Donn to think straight with this beautiful girl sitting face-to-face and rubbing and grinding on his crotch and those big hard nipples rubbing across his face; it was really "hard" to keep your mind on what you were trying to accomplish.

As the night progressed, Preacher seemed to get more nervous; after all he was preaching part time. The three were sitting at the bar when this light-skinned black girl came out and did her dance in front of Phil. She was moving and grinding around and rubbing her breast on Phil's head. I could see the sweat on Preacher's head. He looked like he was fixing to blow! The girl was almost through with her routine. Preacher had stuck $10 in her panties. As she stood straight up in front of him with her sweet spot staring him in the eyes, Preacher screamed and jumped straight back throwing his hands in the air. This was a tall six-foot-five-inch man. Imagine the sight. He loudly yelled, "Ohooo, I gotta get out of here now." He ran for the door yelling, "Get back! Get back." Everybody in the place was so startled. They didn't know what to do. Billy Donn knew this was no time to lose your cool. In this job, you had to keep a level head in extreme circumstances. His training kicked in. He grabbed Grady by the forearm and said, "Sit still for a minute. No time to panic. Something has happened to the preacher." The manager walked around the room to the door with a startled look. Billy and Grady made their way to the door and outside. They could see and hear Preacher running down the sidewalk yelling, "Get back, bulldog. Get back, bulldog!" There was a bulldog chasing Preacher down the sidewalk, growling and snapping at his heels. That big man sure could run. He kept running until he was out of sight. Every so often, he would look back and yell, "Get back, bulldog. Get back!" Grady and Billy Donn went to the car and couldn't believe what was happening.

They finally made radio contact about forty-five minutes later with Preacher and suggested they have a meeting. They had prearranged locations to meet. Billy Donn told him to go to the shack behind the back of an alley. They would meet out of sight. They turned the lights off and eased down the alley. When they walked in the dimly lit small building, they could see the tall preacher man standing in a corner like a scared child.

Billy asked, "What's the matter with you, Preacher? You okay?"

At which time, the big guy said, "Not really," as he was still trying to catch his breath.

Grady asked, "What happened back there?"

Preacher started trying to explain. He said that he got so stirred by that beautiful black girl, but when she stood up over him, all he could see was the devil. He had to escape, run as fast as he could to get away. He said he got down the sidewalk about a block when that bulldog came out of the driveway and started chasing him, and every time, he turned around to see where the bulldog was, he saw the devil's head on that bulldog. "All I could think to do is holler, 'Get back, bulldog. Get back, bulldog. Get back.'"

They finally got him calmed down. Billy Donn said, "Brother man, this is not your kind of gig, but you are a professional law enforcement officer." He knew that Preacher had not been working undercover very long and told him, "You're going to see a lot of things you've never seen before, if you stay in this profession. So we are not going to mention this again outside this room. There is no reason for anyone else to know about this little incident. It wouldn't do any of us any good. It's my decision, and that's the way it's going to be." Billy told Preacher to take the next twenty-four hours off, and they would call him.

The next couple of nights, Billy Donn and Grady worked the Doll House. Same routine. They spotted who they thought was the bad guy, Bobby Longhair, they were after. After all it didn't make sense to stay close to Beth Ann and her work since she was bringing in the money.

After a couple of nights, they went back to the Boobie Trap to get up with what Billy Donn now considered a CI. About nine thirty, she came over and gave the two guys a hug and whispered to Billy, "I've got something for you."

He looked down at her big breast and said, "Am I looking at what you have for me tonight?"

With a sweet little smile, she said, "You can have them later, but I have to tell you something, you silly boy." With that, she winked and walked away.

Later that night while in a dark corner, with her straddling him, she hugged him and whispered that she had decided to burn her boyfriend Bobby Longhair and gave Billy Donn a picture, the guy's name, and date of birth that she slipped in his back pocket for a positive ID. Billy Donn knew then he had the girl's trust and loyalty. He also knew the girl was expecting more from him than he could give her after it all went down. Unfortunately, this was part of the job. Sometimes you get hurt and sometimes others get hurt. This took Billy Donn back to the time he was undercover as a biker. He became close friends to some of the guys in a biker club after he won them over and went through a lot of tough crap to earn his patch, but that is another story!

The next day, the three met at the Sarasota County Sheriff's Office with the state's attorney investigator, Bobby Noles. They went through all the red tape to get a warrant for the dealer. Later that afternoon, the two had the warrant in hand and called Preacher and made all the arrangements with the Sarasota County Sheriff's Office for a raid two nights later at the Doll House.

Billy Donn was getting a little apprehensive about all this coming down to end. He realized that he had been working, but he had almost got too involved with the lifestyle and Beth Ann, though he knew he had a job to do and he was going to do his duty no matter what happens. Billy knew this would possibly be the last night that he would see Beth Ann, at least under these circumstances and probably never again.

The three had gotten together that afternoon to go over the details of the raid that would take place in a couple of nights with Major Perez. Everything had a green light to go. Grady and Billy went back to the hotel to try and rest and relax for a little while. While lying on the bed almost dozing, his cell phone rang. It was Beth Ann. He knew he could not confide in her about what was coming down. You could not trust anyone with this kind of information, not even a CI. He had seen people flip and roll at the last minute for various reasons. They chatted for a little bit and said, "I will see you tonight." They went down to the Bobbie Trap a little later to break up the routine. It was about ten o'clock when they walked in, all three together. They sat down at the bar and ordered a round of beer.

Billy Donn saw Beth Ann giving someone else a lap dance. He felt a little jealous but realized the girl was only trying to make a living at what she knew best. He shoved this thought to the side and finished up the beer watching the other girls dance for a while. Then he saw Beth coming his way. She came over and put her arms around him and her long hair and beautiful breast dropped around him, and she said, "Why are you late? I've missed you. I was worried."

Billy Donn replied, "It's all cool, baby," and she took him over to the corner. He could feel his emotions running high, thinking about this girl and how she might be affected if the bad guy ever found out. The next day, the three men talked and decided that they would try and get her into another town to protect her from the jerk that treated her like crap. Billy knew the people in authority could get this done. He had told her that night before he left to meet him in three days and not to say a word to anyone about coming to meet him out of town. It was all set to go.

The big night finally arrived. They had a big meeting at an undisclosed location with the local sheriff and the Vice and narcotics unit. When the raid went down, they would be arrested along with everyone else and treated no differently to protect their cover.

About one o'clock in the morning, all hell broke loose inside the Doll House as the local boys moved in to serve the warrant on this dirtbag. They all knew he carried a weapon, and so did some of his friends. You always get a little nervous at the last minute, hoping none of your guys get hurt.

Billy had made arrangements with his two guys to cover his back. Grady and Preacher were ready. They knew to stick together. When the lights went up suddenly and the music stopped, the dancing was over. They moved him quickly and swiftly. Suddenly, Billy looked at the dirtbag and saw him going inside his vest and knew what was coming next. He fired at one of the officers and missed. The bad guy was hit with one shot and fell directly to the floor, bleeding profusely. It was the only two shots fired. Everyone was rounded up along with Grady, Preacher, and Billy Donn and taken in and booked. They knew the routine and played along. It was all over. They met a couple of days later at the sheriff's office in Sarasota County. At the meeting, Major Perez advised them that the bad guy was dead. No more dealer for this guy, just justice.

The next day, Billy Donn was off and met Beth Ann at an undisclosed location out of town, near a lake. When she saw Billy Donn, she ran to him and broke down and cried. She said, "I didn't want him to die, Billy."

He told her that's the price you pay when you do what he was doing and that she would be rid of him for the rest of her life and wouldn't have to worry about him anymore. He held the girl as she cried. Feeling remorse for her, Billy Donn said, "Beth Ann, I have strong feelings for you, but you deserve a better life than this. You will have a new start somewhere else. You have an education. Use your head and not just your body. You're a good girl. I won't be able to see you anymore."

With this, she kissed him and told him she would always love him. As she walked away, she stopped and turned around, looked at him, and walked away. Billy Donn never saw or heard from the girl.

Law enforcement in general is a tough job. You lay your life on the line every night that you work, but when you are working deep undercover, you can't even tell your wife, family, or your closest friends what you are doing or where you are at.

For example, a few years after Billy Donn retired, he still had his blue line certificate. He was contacted by an agency from one of the surrounding counties to work undercover as a biker. He had let his hair get long and grew a beard and started hanging around biker bars in the surrounding counties. No one knew what he was doing, not even his closest family. He had ridden motorcycles since he was a kid. So no one thought anything about him riding around on his Harley. He just didn't look like himself as people knew him at a younger age working as a uniformed officer. Everyone knew he had retired and had no idea he was working undercover in another county!

He was off for a few days and had to make a doctor's appointment in Brooksville. When he left the doctor's office, he was very emotional and upset about the news he had gotten. On the way back into town, he could feel the tears running down his face and back into his long hair. He kept it in a ponytail and wore a bandana to play the part. He would never know why, but all he wanted to do was go see his first love, his first wife, and share the information he had found out from his doctor. No one knew what he was really doing. So, when he rode up to her office and got off the Harley looking like a mean-ass biker, it was no wonder the people in the office and Bobbie looked terrified. He walked over to her and asked her if he could talk to her for a minute. She said yes, and the two walked out the door. He could feel the tears running down his face, but he was determined not to break down in front of her. He shared the bad news with her. Bobbie appeared to be very upset and frightened. He would never know if it was the news he gave her or if she seemed to be upset and frightened at his appearance.

He asked, "What's wrong with you?"

She said, "I'm afraid."

"Bobbie, I've always loved you and I always will. There are things that I cannot share with you about what I have been doing for the last year. You'd never understand or believe it with the way I look, even if I could tell you. I'm sorry I frightened you. I don't know why I came straight to you." Billy Donn turned away and got on the bike and roared away down the street with tears streaming down his face. Things were never the same again between Billy Donn and Bobbie after that day.

This is just part of the life of working undercover. Sometimes you sacrifice your friends or sometimes your wife, and there are sometimes you might sacrifice your life!

But he knew under no circumstances could he ever tell her or the children about this part of his life. Fearing they could be killed by the friends of Billy Longhair down south. He would carry the hurt of seeing his former wife turn and walk away in fear. He would take this secret to his grave rather than take a chance of her or the children being put in harm's way.

There were two things that he really enjoyed. One was flying and the other was riding his Harley. A few years later in North Carolina, after slaying the dragon a few times, he decided to take a ride up the parkway one day. At 3,500 feet, it gets a little chilly, and he came off the parkway down toward Soco Falls. The roads were treacherous. He overrode a large sweeping curve at Soco Falls, crashed into the mountain, and woke up under the motorcycle. At that time, he didn't realize how bad the injuries were but wound up with a fractured neck, fractured lower spine, and a sprained ankle.

It ended forty-four years of riding motorcycle and would never work undercover again because of his injuries.

This story is dedicated to all the men and women who work undercover day and night all over this country. A secret must be kept!

ABOUT THE AUTHOR

Jeff Duval was born in Apalachicola, Florida. He lived in Brooksville, Florida, from the age of five for sixty-three years. He married his high school sweetheart, and they were blessed with two sons, Jeffery P. Duval II and Avery L. Duval.

He started his law enforcement career in 1968 by volunteering as a dispatcher at the Hernando County Sheriff's Office under Sheriff Sim L. Lowman and served the citizens of Hernando County for sixteen years. He served twelve of those years under Sheriff Melvin R. Kelly. He served three years in Sumter County under Sheriff Jamie Adams.

In 1988, he was offered a job in Gulf County, Florida, as lieutenant, third in command, until approximately 1995. He retired in 1995 after nearly being beaten to death by two drug dealers. He spent several weeks in a Bay County Hospital. He retired at the recommendation of his doctors, family, and friends.

Jeff was the first marine patrol officer in Hernando County. He was also the founder and first elected president of the Hernando County Sheriff's Mounted Posse and Search and Rescue. Also, in 1976–1977, Jeff was the first deputy to start a pilot program for a motorcycle unit in Hernando County.

While serving in Hernando County, Jeff worked with the Youth Cadet Program. He also spent a lot of his own time and money starting fundraisers for three different children stricken with cancer. He promoted benefit fundraisers for children with cancer that were sent to St. Jude's Hospital.

In the early 1980s, while serving in Sumter County, Florida, he was appointed by Sheriff Jamie Adams to head the Sheriff's Auxiliary Program.

Jeff was assigned to provide security for Clyde Melvin, a triple murder case, at the Gulf County Courthouse in Gulf County, Florida. He was also assigned security for Gov. Bob Martinez when he visited Sheriff Al Harrison to congratulate him on changing from Democrat to Republican.

He loved serving and protecting the good people in the State of Florida.

Jeff suffered PTSD and physical injuries for the rest of his life. He will continue to enjoy the rest of his life enjoying his small ranch a few miles north of Ocala in Levy County. He was a "self-made man"!

FLORIDA CRACKER